BELIEVE

HENRY GALIO

ABOUT THE AUTHOR

Henry Galio writes books that make readers think, laugh, cry, and wonder—more than 40 titles spanning science education, children's stories, holiday adventures, comedy, thriller, horror, romance, and literary fiction.

By day, Henry works in enterprise technology. By night, he writes stories that celebrate curiosity, embrace differences, and explore what it means to be human.

He writes best when it's raining, or snowing, and at night.

To discuss writing, offer feedback and suggestions, or request new stories, email him at: galiowritesnow@gmail.com

CONTENTS

CHAPTER 1
"THE NUMBERS DON'T LIE"

~

December 23rd, 9:00 AM - Santa's Office

The lamplight was warm and golden—the exact color of Christmas morning, if Christmas morning could be distilled into illumination and poured into a brass fixture that had been burning in this same spot since 1847.

Santa's hands rested on the ledger. Not just a ledger, but THE ledger —the master record of names and wishes and small kindnesses observed. His hands were weathered, mapped with lines like ancient trade routes, each crease holding some memory of a child's face lighting up, a parent's grateful tears, a moment when belief became real.

These hands had wrapped presents for Marie Curie. Had left a wooden train for a young Walt Disney. Had placed a journal on the nightstand of a girl named Anne Bradstreet, along with a note that said simply: *Your words matter. Keep writing.*

He touched the paper. The texture was right—rough enough to feel real, smooth enough to write on. The smell of old books and older promises filled his office. Outside the window, snow fell in that particular way it only falls at the North Pole, where the flakes seem to understand they're part of something magical and fall accordingly.

Santa exhaled. Steam rose from his coffee—Mrs. Claus had brought it exactly seventeen minutes ago, which meant it was still the perfect temperature. After four hundred years of marriage, she had timing down to a science. Or maybe it was magic. He'd stopped asking which.

He picked up his pen. Fountain pen, naturally. He'd tried ballpoints once in 1952 and hated everything about them. The scratch of nib on paper was half the joy of the work.

Timothy Henderson, age 7, Des Moines. Wants: LEGO Star Wars set. Needs: His parents to stop fighting in front of him.

Santa made a note. The LEGO set was easy. The other thing... well. That required a different kind of magic. Maybe he'd leave them that photo from their honeymoon, the one still in the attic. Sometimes people just needed to remember.

Sarah Martinez, age 34, San Antonio. Wants: Five minutes of silence. Needs: To know she's doing a good job.

He smiled. Parents never put themselves on the list. But he saw them anyway. Sarah would get the spa certificate—and a note. Just four words. But the right four words.

The office was exactly as it should be. Oak desk, worn smooth by centuries. Globe in the corner (he still used it, even though GPS was supposedly more accurate—the globe had soul). Stacks of letters from children, each one read, each one answered in some way, even if not with words.

The creak of floorboards. The weight of responsibility. The smell of pine and cinnamon and old magic.

This was Christmas. This was the work. This was—

The door exploded open.

"SANTA!"

Jinglebert burst in like a small green tornado wearing an ELF UNIVERSITY sweatshirt and carrying a tablet that glowed with cold blue light. The glow cut through the warm lamplight like a knife through gingerbread.

Santa looked up slowly. "Jinglebert. Deep breaths."

"No time for breathing! We have a CRISIS!" The young elf—89 years old, which in elf years made him roughly 23 and painfully enthusiastic—thrust the tablet forward. "Look at the NUMBERS!"

Santa squinted at the screen. He'd gotten reading glasses in 2019, which had been a humbling experience. Apparently even magical beings weren't immune to presbyopia.

"I'm looking at... lines? Colorful lines that go down?"

"ENGAGEMENT METRICS!" Jinglebert vibrated like a soda can shaken too hard. "We're DROPPING, Santa! Across every demographic!"

"Demo-what-ic?"

"KIDS, Santa! Kids aren't engaging with us anymore!" Jinglebert swiped frantically. "Look—letter writing is down 34% since last year. Website visits to NiceList.com are down 67%—and Santa, have you SEEN our website lately? It's from 1997! Comic Sans font! Dancing snowflakes! The links don't even work anymore!"

Santa blinked. "I thought the dancing snowflakes were charming."

"They were! In 1997! Now they just look... sad!" Jinglebert pulled up another graph. "The average age of disbelief has dropped from 10 years old to SEVEN, Santa. Seven!"

Santa removed his glasses. Rubbed the bridge of his nose. The gesture did nothing to ease the tightness forming in his chest—a slow constriction, like someone was very gently wrapping Christmas lights around his ribs and pulling them taut. He put the glasses back on because the numbers were still there and he needed to see them clearly.

"Thirty-four percent," he repeated slowly.

"And that's just letters! Physical letters!" Jinglebert pulled up another graph. This one was red, which Santa instinctively understood meant bad. "Kids aren't checking the Nice List website anymore. Do you know what they ARE doing?"

"...Playing outside?"

"HA! No! They're on TikTok, Santa! They're asking ALEXA about you! Not YOU—an ALGORITHM!" Jinglebert's voice cracked slightly. "Last week, a kid in Ohio asked Alexa if Santa was real. You know what Alexa said?"

Santa waited.

"'Based on available evidence, Santa Claus is a fictional character created for—'"

"I get the idea."

"DO YOU THOUGH?!" Jinglebert was fully spiraling now. "Because it gets WORSE! Kids are starting to think YOU'RE AI!"

Santa blinked. "I'm... what?"

"Artificial intelligence! They think you're not real! They think you're just... just an algorithm! A chatbot! A deepfake!" Jinglebert pulled up what appeared to be social media posts. "Look—'my parents are definitely Santa, adults are so dumb' with twelve thousand likes. 'Santa isn't real, it's just Amazon with extra steps' with forty-eight thousand likes. 'if santa was real he'd have an instagram' with—"

"What's an instagram?"

Jinglebert made a noise like a small engine dying. "That's... that's EXACTLY the problem, Santa."

Santa looked at the tablet. At the graphs and numbers and engagement metrics. The words meant something, he supposed. Numbers always meant something.

But what they FELT like was...

The tightness in his chest spread. Down his arms. Into his hands—those same hands that had written Anne Bradstreet's name, that had touched millions of gifts, that carried seventeen hundred years of belief in their lines. Now they felt heavy. Foreign.

Like they belonged to someone the world had stopped believing in.

"So what you're telling me," Santa said slowly, and his voice sounded far away even to himself, "is that children... don't believe in me anymore?"

"Not ALL children! But... yeah. Mostly. I mean, statistically speaking—"

"Jinglebert."

"Yes?"

"Statistics are not my language." Santa set the tablet down carefully. As if it might explode. Which, emotionally, it kind of had. "Speak plainly. What's happening?"

Jinglebert took a breath. When he spoke again, his voice was softer. Almost sad.

"The world changed, Santa. It changed fast. Kids grow up with screens now. Everything they see can be edited, filtered, faked. They're seven years old and they already know about deepfakes and CGI and AI-generated content. So when they hear about a magical man who knows if they've been bad or good..."

"They think I'm just another effect," Santa finished quietly.

"Yeah."

Silence filled the office. The lamplight suddenly seemed dimmer. Or maybe that was just Santa's imagination. Or maybe lamplight couldn't compete with the cold truth of a glowing screen.

"I've been doing this for seventeen hundred years," Santa said, and his voice had the quality of old wood—solid, weathered, still strong but bearing the weight of centuries. "I've delivered presents through plagues and wars and industrial revolutions. I adapted to chimneys. To apartments. To smart home security systems that really should have a 'Santa exemption' setting."

A small smile. Then it faded.

"But I've never had to prove I'm real before. Children just... believed. Because belief was the point. The magic was in the not-knowing-for-certain but choosing-to-believe-anyway."

Jinglebert nodded. Waited.

"And now?" Santa asked.

"Now they need proof. Or they need... something. I don't know what. But Santa, if we don't figure it out..." Jinglebert pulled up one more graph. "Next year, we're projected to lose another 40%. In five years, we'll be in single-digit belief metrics among the key 6-12 demographic."

"Stop calling children demographics."

"Sorry. But you see my point?"

Santa did. Unfortunately.

He stood slowly. His knees made a small sound of protest—another humbling development of the last century. Walked to the window. Placed one hand on the cold glass.

Below, the village spread out in perfect Christmas-card formation. Workshop with smoke curling from chimneys. Stables where the reindeer were probably arguing about who got to lead this year (it was always Rudolph, but the others enjoyed the debate). Mrs. Claus's kitchen, where something was baking that made the whole compound smell like comfort and four centuries of knowing exactly what he needed before he asked.

And in the courtyard: young elves. Maybe thirty of them. Taking their lunch break.

Every single one staring at a phone.

Not one looking up.

Not at the workshop. Not at the smoke from the chimneys. Not at the fat, perfect snowflakes falling like God's own confetti.

Not at the magic happening right in front of them.

Santa's hand tightened on the window frame. The cold seeped through the glass into his palm, but he didn't move. Just watched. Those young elves, bathed in blue phone-glow, shoulders hunched, thumbs scrolling.

"They're not looking up," he said quietly.

"What?"

"The young elves. They're not looking at the stars. They're not building snowmen. They're..." He gestured helplessly. "They're staring at screens. Looking for magic in pixels when it's falling on their heads."

Jinglebert came to stand beside him. Looked down at his fellow elves. His tablet-holding, metric-tracking, engagement-measuring generation.

"Yeah," Jinglebert said softly. "We are."

They stood together in silence. Santa's lamplight-warm office and Jinglebert's screen-cold reality, existing in the same space, not quite sure how to reconcile.

Then—

One elf looked up.

Just one.

A young female elf with bright red hair. She'd been scrolling, same as the others, but something made her stop. Lift her head. Tilt her face to the sky.

She pointed.

At what, Santa couldn't tell. Maybe a particularly perfect snowflake. Maybe a bird. Maybe just... up. Just the act of LOOKING up instead of down.

And like a ripple: the others looked too.

One by one, they lifted their heads. Followed her finger. Saw whatever she was seeing—or maybe just saw that there was something worth seeing beyond their screens.

The phones lowered. Just for a moment. Just for that one pointing finger and the curiosity it sparked.

Santa felt something in his chest unclench. Just slightly.

"Maybe," he said quietly, "they're not lost. Maybe they're just... looking in different directions. And maybe I need to learn to wave from where they're actually looking."

Jinglebert turned sharply. "So... are you saying...?"

Santa took a breath. Let it out slowly. The steam of it fogged the window briefly before fading, leaving just the scene below: young elves slowly returning to their phones, but different now. Changed by that one moment of looking up.

"What do you propose?" Santa asked.

Jinglebert's face lit up like a Christmas tree plugged in for the first time in December. "Seriously?"

"You came in here with graphs and metrics and 'crisis' energy. You must have a solution."

"I do! I mean, I might! I mean, I have IDEAS!" Jinglebert's enthusiasm rebooted instantly. He pulled up his tablet again. "We need to meet them where they are, Santa. We need digital presence. Social media. Verified accounts. We need—and don't freak out when I say this—we need to go VIRAL."

"Viral," Santa repeated. "Like a disease?"

"No! Well, sort of! But good viral! We need Instagram, TikTok, maybe Twitter—well, it's called X now, but nobody really uses that name— and definitely YouTube Shorts and—"

"Jinglebert."

"Yes?"

"I don't understand any of those words."

"They're PLATFORMS, Santa! Places where people share content! We could show them the workshop! The reindeer! The actual magic! Give them PROOF that you're real!"

Santa turned from the window. Looked at the young elf. At his enthusiasm. His genuine desire to help. His tablet with its cold blue glow and its promising solutions.

"And you think," Santa said slowly, "that showing them the workshop will make them believe?"

"Yes! Transparency builds trust! If they can SEE the magic—"

"Magic revealed is magic destroyed, Jinglebert."

The words hung in the air. Heavy. Ancient. True.

Jinglebert opened his mouth. Closed it. The tablet dimmed slightly in his hands, as if even technology understood it had been outmatched by something older.

"But," Jinglebert said carefully, "what if hiding the magic is also destroying it? What if they need to see SOMETHING? Not everything —just... enough to know you're not an algorithm?"

Santa walked back to his desk. Sat heavily. These conversations used to be easier. Used to be about toy production schedules and reindeer feeding times. Now they were about... what? Proving his own existence?

"Not if we control the narrative! Not if we show them just enough to—"

"To what? To prove myself?" Santa's voice wasn't angry. Just tired. The kind of tired that accumulates over centuries of the same work, the same love, suddenly being questioned. "When did I become something that needs proving?"

Jinglebert opened his mouth. Closed it. Opened it again.

"I don't know, Santa. But somewhere between radio and TikTok, something changed. And we either change with it or we become... we become what the history books are for future kids. A story their parents used to believe."

The words hung in the air like ornaments. Pretty. Fragile. Devastatingly true.

Santa looked at his hands. Those same hands. Marie Curie. Walt Disney. Anne Bradstreet. Billions of names written in careful script. Seventeen hundred years of seeing people—really SEEING them— when the world looked past them.

At the ledger. At the list of names and needs and wishes that only he could see because only he had spent seventeen centuries learning to look.

Timothy Henderson needs his parents to remember why they fell in love.

Sarah Martinez needs to know she's doing a good job.

Kevin Patterson, age 42, needs to know someone sees his grief.

He knew them. All of them. Every single one.

But they didn't know him anymore.

They thought he was AI.

"Show me," Santa said finally.

"Show you what?"

"These platforms. These... viral things. Show me what you're proposing."

Jinglebert's face lit up like a Christmas tree. "REALLY?!"

"I'm not promising anything. But show me. Explain it. Help me understand what you think we should do."

"Oh Santa, you won't regret this! I've actually already mocked up some content strategies and—wait, you're not going to like this—I already secured a handle on Instagram! It's @NaughtyOrNice! Perfect, right? I mean, I didn't want to assume, but I wanted to be READY if you said yes, and—"

"Jinglebert."

"Yes?"

"You secured a handle before asking permission?"

"...Is that bad?"

Santa should have been annoyed. Should have given the young elf a lecture about overstepping. Should have—

He laughed.

It surprised him. A real laugh. From the belly. The kind of laugh that reminded him why he'd been doing this for seventeen hundred years. Because young people were audacious. Because hope was presumptuous. Because belief—real belief—didn't ask permission. It just acted.

"You've got initiative, kid. I'll give you that." He stood, walked around the desk, put a hand on Jinglebert's shoulder. "Alright. You've got my attention. Tomorrow morning, you show me this brave new world of social media. We'll see if an old man can learn new tricks."

"You're not old! You're... chronologically experienced!"

"I'm seventeen hundred years old, Jinglebert. That's old in any time-zone." Santa squeezed the elf's shoulder. "But maybe that's the point. Maybe I need to remember that the world keeps turning. Children keep growing. And magic... magic has to evolve too."

He walked back to the window. The young elves were mostly back on their phones now. But that one—the red-haired one who'd pointed— she was still looking at the sky. Still seeing whatever she'd seen. And two others had joined her, phones pocketed, faces tilted up.

"Maybe," Santa said quietly, "they're not lost. Maybe they're just... looking in different directions. And maybe I need to learn to wave from where they're actually looking."

Jinglebert came to stand beside him again. "So we're doing this?"

Santa took a breath. Let it out slowly. The steam of it fogged the window briefly before fading.

"We're considering it," he corrected. "Let me talk to Mrs. Claus tonight. She's been steering this sleigh through rough weather for four hundred years—I'm not making this call without her compass. If she thinks I won't completely embarrass myself—"

"You won't!"

"—then tomorrow, we'll discuss this properly. With cookies. And cocoa. And realistic expectations about an old man's ability to understand 'engagement metrics.'"

"DEAL!" Jinglebert practically bounced. "Oh Santa, this is going to be AMAZING! We're going to reach SO many kids! The analytics are going to be—"

"Jinglebert."

"Yeah?"

"Less talk. More cookies. Have Mrs. Claus send up a plate. And tell her..." he paused, "tell her I'll need to talk tonight. She'll know what I mean."

"On it!" Jinglebert raced for the door, then paused. Turned back. "Hey Santa?"

"Yes?"

"Thanks. For listening. I know this is weird. I know it's scary. But... I really think it could help. I really think we could reach them again."

Santa nodded slowly. "I hope you're right."

The door closed. The office returned to its lamplight quiet.

Santa sat at his desk. Looked at the ledger. At his list of names and needs.

Then, despite himself, he pulled the tablet closer. Squinted at the screen.

@NaughtyOrNice

The handle sat there. Waiting. Empty. Like a wrapped present that hadn't been opened yet. Ready to be filled with... what? Proof? Presence? Performance?

He thought about the children on their phones. Not looking at stars.

He thought about the young elves in the courtyard. Until one pointed up. Until the others followed.

He thought about the question Jinglebert hadn't actually asked but that hung in the office like smoke from a chimney:

How do you prove you're real to a world that doesn't believe in real anymore?

Santa closed the tablet. Opened the ledger.

Picked up his pen—the one he'd used for seventeen hundred years, the one that had written Marie Curie's name and Walt Disney's name and Anne Bradstreet's name.

And wrote the next name on the list.

Because that's what he'd always done. That's what he'd always BE.

Real or not real. Believed or not believed. Viral or invisible.

He knew their names. He saw their needs.

That was the magic.

Everything else was just... delivery method.

"We'll see," he whispered to the lamplight. "We'll see."

Outside, snow continued falling. The elves went back to their phones, but three still looked at the sky, fingers pointed at something worth seeing.

And in his office, Santa Claus—1,700 years old, deeply uncertain, but willing to try—took a breath and stepped toward tomorrow.

Even if tomorrow spoke in engagement metrics and required learning what the hell an "instagram" was.

The work continued.

It always did.

CHAPTER 2
"MRS. CLAUS WEIGHS IN"

~

December 23rd, 11:30 AM - The Kitchen

The kitchen smelled like every good memory Santa had ever carried down a chimney.

Cinnamon. Brown sugar. Butter melting into flour. Ginger root and vanilla extract. The particular scent of something being created with care—not magic, exactly, but the kind of alchemy that happens when you've been baking for four hundred years and your hands know the dough better than they know their own lines.

Mrs. Claus—Martha, though only Santa called her that anymore—stood at the counter with her arms buried to the elbows in bread dough. Her hair was pinned back with the efficiency of someone who'd been doing this since before hairpins were invented. Flour dusted her apron in abstract patterns that would've made Jackson Pollock jealous.

Her hands moved in that particular rhythm—push, fold, turn, push, fold, turn—that had nothing to do with thinking and everything to do with processing. This was how she thought. How she worked through problems. How she'd worked through every major decision in four centuries of marriage.

The dough would tell her what to do. Eventually.

She heard him before she saw him. The particular heaviness of his footsteps. Not the tired-after-work heaviness. The weighed-down-by-thoughts heaviness.

"How long?" she asked without looking up.

"How long what?"

"How long have you been standing in the doorway trying to decide if you want to talk about it or brood about it?"

A pause. "...Thirty seconds."

"Closer to two minutes." She finally looked up. Saw his face. "Ah. Jinglebert showed you the metrics."

"You knew?"

"Darling, I've been married to you for four hundred years. You think I don't know when a young elf with too much enthusiasm and a tablet is going to give you an existential crisis?" She gestured to the table with a flour-covered hand. "Sit. I'll make you cocoa."

"I don't need—"

"Sit."

He sat.

The chair creaked under his weight. It was his chair—had been since 1823. She'd tried to get him to let the workshop elves make a new one, but he'd refused. Said this one had character. Said it knew him.

She understood that. Her rolling pin was from 1642 and she'd stab anyone who tried to replace it.

She kept kneading while milk heated on the stove. The kitchen was enormous—had to be, to produce cookies for a global operation—but this corner was hers. Smaller. Warmer. More human-scaled. The industrial ovens were in the next room. Here, everything was wood and copper and the gentle chaos of a workspace that had evolved organically over centuries.

Mason jars of ingredients lined the shelves. Recipe cards in her handwriting, going back decades. Some in languages that weren't spoken anymore. A photograph from 1952—her and Kris at the radio station, both looking terrified. She kept it as a reminder that they'd survived changes before.

"Talk to me," she said, not looking at him. Looking would make him self-conscious. The dough was easier to talk to.

"Jinglebert says we're losing them."

"The children?"

"They think I'm AI, Martha. Artificial intelligence. They think I'm... generated. Fake. A chatbot with a sleigh."

She heard the wound in his voice. The particular kind of hurt that came from being disbelieved after seventeen hundred years of showing up.

"And what did Jinglebert propose?" she asked, though she already knew. The young elves had been talking about this for months. She just wanted to hear it from Kris.

"Social media. Instagram. TikTok. Going..." he made air quotes with his fingers, something he'd learned from a teenager in 2019 and still couldn't do without looking awkward, "...viral."

"Mm."

"That's it? Just 'mm'?"

"I'm thinking." Push, fold, turn. "You said the same thing about radio in 1952."

Santa was quiet for a moment. Then: "That was different."

"Was it?"

"Radio was... radio was one broadcast. One night. I could control it. This is... everything. All the time. Everywhere."

"True." She shaped the dough into a ball, covered it with a clean towel. Set it aside to rise. Moved to the stove. "But the fear was the same."

She poured milk into two mugs. Added cocoa powder—the good stuff, from a small chocolatier in Belgium who didn't know she was his best customer. A pinch of cinnamon. A drop of vanilla. Stirred with a cinnamon stick because some things should be done right even when they're simple.

She brought both mugs to the table. Sat across from him. Her own chair, smaller, with a cushion she'd embroidered herself in 1897 when she'd been angry about something she couldn't even remember now.

"Tell me about 1952," she said.

"You were there."

"Tell me anyway."

He wrapped his hands around the mug. Steam rose between them like a ghost of Christmas past.

"We were trying to be modern," he said slowly. "Television was new. Radio was everywhere. The young elves said we needed to 'embrace the medium.' Said children were listening to radio shows instead of reading letters. Said we were losing relevance."

"Sound familiar?"

"...Yes."

"And what happened?"

A rueful smile. "I announced on air that Timmy Henderson was getting the red bicycle. Except there were two Timmy Hendersons in the same town. Both had asked for red bicycles. I got the addresses mixed up."

"And?"

"And Christmas morning, one Timmy got the right bicycle. The other Timmy got a dictionary because that's what I'd planned for the other house. Both Timmys were confused. Both sets of parents were angry. The local paper ran a story: 'Santa Gets It Wrong: Radio Stunt Backfires.'"

"But you fixed it," Martha prompted.

"I went back that night. With the right bicycle. And an apology letter. And a new dictionary for the first Timmy because by then he'd gotten attached to it." Santa took a sip of cocoa. Perfect temperature. She always knew. "Both Timmys wrote me thank-you letters the next year. Said it was the best Christmas ever because Santa came back."

Martha waited.

"You're saying I'll make mistakes with this too," Santa said.

"I'm saying you made mistakes with radio and learned from them. You made mistakes with television—remember the 1964 incident?"

"The commercial? Don't remind me."

"You were horrified that Christmas was becoming 'too commercial.' Refused to appear in any advertisements. Then watched toy companies use knockoff Santas who didn't care about the kids, just the profits."

"And?"

"And you learned that being part of the conversation was better than letting others define you." She reached across the table. Put her hand over his. "The medium changes, Kris. The message doesn't. You've been showing up for seventeen hundred years. You've adapted to chimneys, apartments, security systems, and children who don't leave cookies because they're gluten-free now."

"But social media—"

"Is different. Yes. It's instant. It's everywhere. It's performative. But darling..." She squeezed his hand. "So is Christmas. It always has been. The performance of generosity. The performance of belief. The public ritual that carries private meaning."

He looked up at her. Those old, kind eyes that had seen so much and still chose to see the good.

"What if I fail?" he asked quietly. "What if I go online and they still don't believe? What if proof isn't enough? What if—"

The kitchen door exploded open.

A small elf covered head-to-toe in flour stumbled in, arms windmilling, clearly having just escaped some kind of baking catastrophe.

"MRS. CLAUS!" the elf yelled. "THE GINGERBREAD HOUSE COLLAPSED! AGAIN! I TOLD THEM THE WALLS NEEDED MORE SUPPORT BUT NOOO, EVERYONE WANTED TO USE THE PRETTY ICING, AND NOW WE HAVE THREE THOUSAND COOKIES EVERYWHERE AND—"

She stopped. Saw Santa. Blinked flour out of her eyes.

"Oh. Hi, Santa. Sorry. Bad time?"

"Buttons," Mrs. Claus said calmly. "Deep breath."

The elf—Buttons, named for her tendency to stress-eat cookie buttons off gingerbread men—took a breath. It didn't help much.

"We're SO BEHIND, Mrs. C. Christmas Eve is TOMORROW and we still have twelve thousand cookies to bake and the butter situation is CRITICAL and half the staff is on TikTok instead of working and—"

"Wait," Santa interrupted. "The staff is on what?"

"TikTok!" Buttons gestured wildly. "You know, the app? Where everyone posts videos? The young elves have been doing these... these 'cookie decorating tutorials' and 'a day in the North Pole workshop' videos and apparently they've gone SUPER viral and now they're getting MILLIONS of views and they want to make MORE content instead of MAKING ACTUAL COOKIES—"

Santa and Mrs. Claus exchanged a look.

"The young elves," Santa said slowly, "are already on social media."

"Oh yeah," Buttons said, oblivious to the significance. "Have been for like two years. Some of them have bigger followings than actual celebrities. Snowflake—you know, from Gift Wrapping?—has like five million followers on Instagram. Her 'ASMR wrapping paper sounds' videos are HUGE."

Santa's mouth opened. Closed. Opened again.

"Five million," he repeated.

"Yeah! And Tinsel from Ornament Design does these 'satisfying decoration videos' that get TENS of millions of views! It's actually amazing! People LOVE behind-the-scenes stuff from the North Pole!" Buttons paused. "Wait, did you not know about this?"

"No," Santa said faintly. "I did not know about this."

"Oh." Buttons looked between them. "Is that... bad?"

"No," Mrs. Claus said quickly. "It's fine, dear. Now about those cookies—"

"RIGHT! THE COOKIES! So do you want me to abandon the gingerbread house entirely or should we attempt structural reinforcement or maybe we just make it into a modern deconstructed gingerbread situation where the collapse is INTENTIONAL and—"

"Buttons."

"Yes, Mrs. C?"

"Start with the sugar cookies. Simple. Classic. We'll worry about architecture later."

"OKAY!" Buttons spun toward the door, still shedding flour like a small blizzard. Paused at the threshold. "Oh, and Santa? If you do decide to join TikTok, my offer stands—I'll be your social media manager! I've got IDEAS! We could do a whole 'ASMR toy making' series and 'What Santa Eats for Breakfast' content and maybe even a 'Rating Your Cookies' segment where you—"

"Thank you, Buttons. That's... we'll consider it."

"AWESOME!" She disappeared in a cloud of enthusiasm and flour.

The kitchen returned to quiet.

Santa stared at the door. Then at Martha.

"The elves have been doing this for two years."

"Apparently."

"And I didn't know."

"You've been busy. Seventeen hundred years of tradition doesn't run itself." She sipped her cocoa. "But yes. The world changed. The young ones adapted. And we... we're just noticing now."

Santa leaned back in his chair. It creaked sympathetically.

"I'm old," he said.

"You're experienced."

"I'm out of touch."

"You're focused on what matters—the children, the magic, the work. That's not out of touch. That's committed." She set down her mug. Leaned forward. "But Kris, darling, here's the thing: commitment without adaptation becomes stubbornness. And stubbornness becomes irrelevance."

He looked at her. Really looked. Saw the lines around her eyes—earned through smiles and worries and four hundred years of keeping Christmas running behind the scenes. Saw the strength in her flour-dusted hands. Saw the woman who'd been his partner through every change, every challenge, every moment when he'd wondered if he could keep going.

"What do you think I should do?" he asked.

She pulled the bread from earlier out of its warm corner—it had risen perfectly, the way dough always did when you gave it time and attention. Set it on the table between them. Still fragrant. Still warm. The simple magic of flour and water becoming something more.

"I think," she said carefully, laying her hands flat on the table, "that you should do what you've always done: show up. Be present. Be honest. Be YOU."

She paused. Met his eyes.

"Do it your way, Kris. Honest. Real. No algorithms manipulating your message. No performance for the sake of performance. Just you. Just the work you've always done. Just... let them see it this time."

"But if they don't believe—"

"Kris." Her voice was soft but firm. "You're afraid they won't believe. But darling... they're DESPERATE to believe. They just don't know how anymore. The world has taught them that everything is fake, everything is an effect, everything is selling them something. They've forgotten how to recognize real when they see it."

She reached across the table again, took both his hands in hers.

"Show them," she said. "Show them what real looks like. What service without performance looks like. What love without expectation of return looks like."

"And if they still don't believe?" His voice cracked slightly. "If they call me fake? AI? A fraud? If they—"

"Then you do the work anyway." Her grip tightened. "The work is the point, Kris. Not the applause. Not the likes. Not the proof of your own reality. The WORK. Seeing the children. Knowing their names. Showing up."

She smiled, and in that smile was four hundred years of watching him wrestle with this same fear in different forms.

"You taught me that, remember? Back in 1623? When I asked why you kept leaving gifts for the cobbler's children even though their father was a drunk who'd never thank you?" She squeezed his hands. "You said: 'Because the work isn't about being seen. It's about SEEING them. Witnessing. Knowing someone's name when the world forgets. That's the magic.'"

Santa stared at their joined hands. Hers still dusted with flour. His weathered and old and carrying seventeen hundred years of gift-giving.

"I said that?"

"You did. And you've lived it every day since." She pulled back, released his hands, gestured at the bread. "Break bread with me. Then go tell Jinglebert you'll do this thing. On your terms. Your way."

He picked up the bread. Tore it in half. Steam rose from the soft interior. Handed her half. They ate in silence—the communion of old marriages, where words were optional and presence was enough.

Finally, Santa spoke.

"Christmas Eve morning," he said quietly. "We launch."

Martha's face split into a smile. "You're sure?"

"No. But I'm willing. And maybe that's enough." He stood, walked around the table, kissed the top of her head. She smelled like cinnamon and patience and four hundred years of being his compass. "Thank you."

"For what?"

"For reminding me why I started this in the first place." He paused at the door, one hand on the frame. "And for always steering me back to north when I forget which way is true."

"That's what four hundred years of marriage is for, dear." She was already moving back to her counter, where new dough waited. "Now go. I have to help Buttons prevent a cookie apocalypse. And you have a list to finish."

He moved to leave. Stopped. Turned back.

"Martha?"

"Yes?"

"What if I make a fool of myself?"

She smiled. The same smile he'd fallen in love with in 1623 when she'd been a baker's daughter and he'd been a mysterious man with a sleigh who kept stealing her cookies for "delivery purposes."

"Then you'll be a fool who tried. Which is better than being a wise man who stayed silent." She turned back to her work, hands already finding their rhythm. "Now go. Christmas waits for no one. Not even you."

He left, letting the door swing closed behind him.

Mrs. Claus stood in her kitchen, hands returning to the dough, and allowed herself one moment of worry.

Not about Instagram or TikTok or social media.

But about her husband's heart.

She'd watched him carry the weight of Christmas for centuries. Watched him internalize every lost letter, every disappointed child, every moment when belief wavered. Watched him blame himself for things that weren't his fault—the passage of time, the change in culture, the simple truth that children grew up.

And now he was about to put himself online. To expose himself to the whole world's opinion. To make himself vulnerable to every troll, every skeptic, every person who'd already decided that magic was dead and Santa was just a corporate mascot.

It would hurt him. She knew that.

But maybe... maybe it would also remind him why he'd started this in the first place.

Not to be believed.

Not to be praised.

Not even to be seen.

But to SEE. To witness. To know the names and needs of children who thought they were invisible.

That was the magic.

Everything else was just wrapping paper.

She returned to kneading, and in the rhythm of her hands, she found her prayer:

Let him remember. Let him see what matters. Let him know that proving himself isn't the point—showing up is.

And outside the kitchen, through walls and windows and the particular magic that bound them together, Santa felt that prayer like warmth on his skin.

He stood in the hallway for a moment. Put his hand over his heart.

"I hear you," he whispered to his wife, to himself, to the magic that had always been bigger than both of them.

Then he went back to his office.

To his list.

To his work.

Tomorrow would bring social media and Jinglebert's enthusiasm and the terrifying prospect of learning what a "hashtag" was.

But today?

Today he still had names to write.

Needs to notice.

Magic to deliver.

One child at a time.

The way he'd always done it.

The way it had always mattered.

CHAPTER 3
"THE OLD GUARD RESISTS"

～

December 23rd, 2:00 PM - Workshop Floor

The workshop floor smelled like woodsmoke and possibility.

Sawdust hung in the air like tiny snowflakes that had forgotten how to fall. The smell of fresh pine mixed with paint and glue and that particular scent of creativity—sharp and sweet and slightly chaotic. Every surface held half-finished toys: wooden trains waiting for wheels, stuffed bears waiting for eyes, remote-control cars waiting for someone to figure out why they only turned left.

This was where Christmas was made. Not in the office with ledgers and lists. Not in the kitchen with cookies and comfort. Here. On the floor. With hands and tools and the kind of magic that looked suspiciously like hard work if you watched long enough.

Santa stood in the center of it all, surrounded by his senior staff.

Torbin was there—head toymaker, 347 years old, arms like tree trunks from decades of hammering and shaping and refusing to let the machines do everything. His apron was covered in sawdust patterns that told the story of his day: a dollhouse here, a wooden sword there, a train set somewhere around his left pocket.

Greta stood beside him—stable master, 412 years old, smelling like hay and reindeer and the particular kind of patience you need to manage flying animals with opinions. Her hands were never quite clean, always bearing traces of oats or leather polish or the special mixture she used to keep hooves healthy at high altitudes.

Jinglebert bounced on his toes near the back, tablet glowing, barely containing his enthusiasm.

Mrs. Claus leaned against a workbench, arms crossed, watching everything with that particular awareness of someone who knew exactly how this would go and was prepared to intervene at the right moment.

And by the stable door, visible through the open archway that connected workshop to stables, Rudolph stood in shadow. His red nose glowed softly—not bright, just... present. Like a warning light that had learned to be subtle.

The young elves had gathered at the edges. Thirty or forty of them, phones tucked away but clearly eager. They'd heard rumors. They knew something big was happening.

Santa cleared his throat.

The workshop sounds didn't stop immediately—saws kept sawing, hammers kept hammering, 3D printers kept printing (Torbin hated those things but even he admitted they were useful for the complicated stuff). But conversations died down. Attention shifted.

"Thank you all for coming," Santa began. "I know we're in crunch time. Christmas Eve is tomorrow. But this affects everyone, so I wanted to be transparent."

Torbin's eyebrow raised at the word "transparent." It wasn't a word Santa used often.

"Jinglebert has brought to my attention that we're facing a... let's call it a relevance problem. Children aren't engaging with us the way they used to. Belief metrics—" he stumbled slightly over the phrase, "—are declining. So we're considering a new approach."

He gestured to Jinglebert.

The young elf practically vibrated forward, tablet blazing.

"Hi everyone! Okay, so, EXCITING NEWS!" Jinglebert swiped through screens like a tiny green DJ. "We're going to establish digital presence! Instagram, TikTok, maybe YouTube! We're going to show the world the REAL North Pole! Behind-the-scenes content, day-in-the-life videos, maybe even livestream some of the delivery run on Christmas Eve!"

The last part landed like a snowball in a library.

Silence.

Complete, heavy, concerned silence.

Torbin spoke first. His voice was like rocks grinding together—solid, immovable, slightly irritated.

"You want to put Christmas on the internet."

"Not ON the internet," Jinglebert corrected quickly. "More like... accessible VIA the internet? We'd be meeting kids where they are! Showing them the magic is real!"

"Magic revealed is magic destroyed," Torbin said flatly.

"Not if we control the narrative! Not if we show them just enough to—"

"There is no 'just enough.'" Torbin turned to Santa. "Sir, with respect, this is a mistake. We've operated in mystery for seventeen hundred years. The moment we start performing for cameras, we become performers. We stop being real and start being content."

Several older elves nodded.

Greta stepped forward. Her voice was softer than Torbin's but no less firm.

"I have concerns about security," she said. "If we're showing the workshop, the stables, the sleigh routes... what's stopping someone from tracking us? From figuring out our patterns? We have magic protecting us, yes, but magic and GPS don't always play nice. What if someone follows the sleigh?"

"We won't show exact routes!" Jinglebert protested. "Just, like, general footage! Establishing shots! Nothing specific!"

"Everything is specific on the internet," Greta countered. "Metadata. Timestamps. Background details. I've seen what people can figure out from a single photograph. They tracked down a flag location from star positions once. You think they can't figure out where Santa's workshop is?"

Murmurs from the crowd. The younger elves looked uncertain now. The older ones looked vindicated.

Mrs. Claus remained silent, watching Santa's face.

Santa held up a hand. "These are fair concerns. Which is why I'm establishing rules. If—and I mean IF—we do this, we do it on our terms."

He counted on his fingers:

"One: No sponsored content. We're not selling anything but belief. No commercials. No partnerships with toy companies. No 'this sleigh brought to you by—' anything."

Nods from the older guard.

"Two: No algorithm manipulation. No tricks. No clickbait. No 'you won't BELIEVE what Santa did next!' We post honest content or we don't post at all."

Jinglebert deflated slightly but nodded.

"Three: Authenticity only. We don't perform for the camera. We don't stage things. We don't... what's the word... curate?"

"Curate," Jinglebert confirmed.

"We don't curate reality. We show what's real. Sawdust and all."

Torbin grunted. Not quite approval, but not disapproval either.

"And four:" Santa's voice became firmer. "We control the narrative. Nobody edits us. Nobody spins us. Nobody tells us what story to tell. We tell our own story. Or we tell no story at all."

The workshop was silent again. But this time it felt different. Less hostile. More... considering.

"What about the delivery?" a young elf called from the back. "Can we livestream that? Kids would LOVE to see the sleigh in action!"

Torbin made a noise like a disgusted walrus.

But Greta looked thoughtful. "If we're careful... if it's just brief clips, nothing that shows locations or timing... it might actually help with the belief problem."

"Or," Torbin countered, "it might turn Christmas into a spectator sport. Watch Santa deliver presents like it's a game. No mystery. No magic. Just... content to consume."

"People used to say that about radio," Mrs. Claus said quietly.

Everyone turned.

She pushed off from the workbench. Walked into the center of the circle.

"1952. Radio broadcast. You all remember." She looked at the older elves. "We said it would cheapen Christmas. Make it commercial. Turn magic into performance."

"And we were right," Torbin said. "That broadcast was a disaster."

"The broadcast was flawed," Mrs. Claus corrected. "But the concept? The concept of meeting children where they were? That wasn't wrong. We learned. We adapted. We got better."

She turned to Santa.

"The question isn't whether this is scary. It is. The question is whether we trust ourselves to do it right. To maintain our integrity while evolving our approach."

Santa met her eyes. Saw the support there. The permission.

"One livestream," he said suddenly. "From the sleigh. Christmas Eve. Brief. General. Nothing specific. Just... proof that we're doing the work. That we're real."

Jinglebert's eyes went wide. "REALLY?!"

"IF," Santa emphasized, "everyone here agrees it can be done safely. I want Greta to clear the security. I want Torbin to make sure the cameras don't interfere with the magic. I want Mrs. Claus to tell me if I'm about to make a fool of myself."

"You're always about to make a fool of yourself, dear," Mrs. Claus said fondly. "That's half your charm."

Light laughter from the crowd.

"So," Santa said, looking around at his team—young and old, enthusiastic and skeptical, digital and analog. "Do we do this? Or do we keep doing what we've always done and hope the children find their way back to us?"

The young elves were nodding eagerly. The older ones looked less certain but not hostile.

Torbin crossed his arms. "If we do this—and I mean IF—I have conditions."

"Name them."

"No filming in the workshop during actual production. We're not performing for cameras while making toys. The work comes first."

"Agreed."

"No posting anything that reveals our magic. We can show results but not methods. Let them see flying reindeer, but don't explain how the flying works."

"Fair."

"And if this turns into a circus—if it stops being about the children and starts being about the followers—we shut it down immediately. No debate. No 'let's give it more time.' Just... done."

Santa nodded slowly. "Deal."

Greta stepped forward. "I'll need to review all footage before it's posted. Security clearance. If I see anything that compromises our location or safety, it gets cut. No arguments."

"Agreed."

Jinglebert was practically glowing. "This is AMAZING! We're going to reach SO many kids! The analytics are going to be—"

"Jinglebert."

"Yes, Santa?"

"The goal isn't metrics. The goal isn't followers. The goal is connection. If a single child feels seen because of what we post? That's success. If ten million people watch and nobody's life changes? That's failure. Understand?"

The young elf sobered. Nodded seriously. "Understood."

"Good. Then let's—"

"No."

The voice came from the stable doorway.

Everyone turned.

Rudolph stepped into the light.

His nose glowed brighter now—not warm and cheerful, but sharp and red and almost angry. His antlers cast shadows on the wall behind him. His eyes held something the others couldn't quite read. Not hostility. Not fear.

Knowledge.

"Rudolph?" Santa said carefully.

The reindeer walked into the center of the circle. He was bigger than people remembered—nine feet tall at the shoulder, muscles built from pulling a sleigh laden with magic across impossible distances. His coat was perfect, his stance powerful.

But his nose... his nose looked tired. Like a light that had been burning too long.

"You can't prove magic," Rudolph said. His voice was deep, patient, sad. "You can try. But you can't."

"We're not trying to prove—" Jinglebert started.

"Yes you are." Rudolph turned his massive head. "That's exactly what you're trying to do. You think if you show them the workshop, the reindeer, the sleigh, they'll believe. But they won't."

"How do you know?" Santa asked gently.

Rudolph's laugh was bitter. "Because I'm already online, Santa. Have been for years. Do you know what they say about my nose?"

Silence.

"They say it's an LED. A light implant. Special effects. CGI. I've seen the videos. Kids filming me during test flights. Posting them. Analyzing them frame by frame. And you know what the top comment is? Every single time?"

He waited.

"'Fake. That's just an LED.'"

The words hung in the air like smoke.

Santa felt something crack in his chest. Not break—crack. Like ice under too much weight. That word. *Fake.* Applied to Rudolph. To magic. To seventeen hundred years of showing up.

His hands—those same hands that had written names for centuries —curled into fists at his sides. Not in anger. In something closer to grief.

"I am a reindeer whose nose glows red," Rudolph continued, his voice steady but strained. "I can fly. I can navigate through any weather. I have been leading this sleigh for seventy-three years. And they think I'm a battery-powered novelty you can buy on Amazon for $12.99."

Several elves shifted uncomfortably. The young ones who'd been so excited—their phones still in their pockets but their enthusiasm visibly dimming. They were looking at Rudolph differently now. Seeing him. Really seeing him. And understanding what they'd been too eager to consider: this would cost something.

"So when you say you're going to 'show them the magic,'" Rudolph said, looking at Santa with those ancient eyes, "I want you to understand something: they will find a way to explain it away. Because that's what people do now. Everything has an explanation. Everything is a trick. Everything is content generated for engagement."

"Then what do we do?" Santa asked, and his voice was genuinely lost. The crack in his chest spreading. "If proof doesn't work, if showing them doesn't work, if—"

"I don't know," Rudolph said simply. "I just know that exposing yourself to disbelief is harder than you think. And once they've explained away your magic, it's very difficult to get it back."

He turned. Walked back toward the stables.

At the doorway, he paused.

"But Santa? If you're going to do it anyway—and I think you should, because doing nothing is worse—just... be prepared. Be prepared for them to still not believe. And be prepared for how that will feel."

Then he was gone.

The workshop was completely silent.

Even the saws had stopped.

Santa stood in the center of his team, feeling the weight of Rudolph's words settle over him like snow. Heavy snow. The kind that accumulates quietly until suddenly you realize you can't move under it.

They would call it fake.

They would explain it away.

They would find reasons not to believe.

And he would have to watch. Would have to read the comments. Would have to carry that disbelief along with everything else he carried.

"Sir?" Jinglebert's voice was small. "Do you... do you still want to do this?"

Santa looked around. At Torbin's skepticism. At Greta's concern. At Mrs. Claus's steady support. At the young elves' hope—diminished now, more sober, but still there. At the space where Rudolph had been.

He thought about seventeen hundred years of showing up.

He thought about children who needed to feel seen.

He thought about the possibility of failure.

And he thought about the certainty of irrelevance if he did nothing.

"Yes," he said finally. "We do this. We try. We risk it. Because Rudolph's right about one thing: doing nothing is worse."

He turned to Jinglebert.

"Tomorrow morning. Christmas Eve. We launch the account. One post. Simple. Honest. No tricks. Just... me. Being me. Doing what I do."

"And the livestream?" Jinglebert asked hopefully.

"One brief moment. During the delivery. Nothing specific. Just... proof that we're doing the work. That we're real." He paused. "Even if they explain it away. Even if they don't believe. We'll have tried."

Mrs. Claus came to stand beside him. Put her hand on his arm.

"We'll try together," she said.

Torbin grunted. "Fine. But the moment this becomes about performance instead of purpose, I'm out."

"Noted," Santa said.

Greta nodded. "I'll review all security protocols tonight. We'll do this carefully or not at all."

"Thank you."

The meeting broke. Elves returned to work. The young ones whispered—not excitedly anymore, but thoughtfully, soberly. The old ones muttered about the end of mystery.

Santa stood in the center of the workshop floor, sawdust swirling around his boots, and felt the weight of tomorrow pressing down. Not just on his shoulders. In his bones. In the particular way exhaustion settles when you've been carrying something heavy for so long you've forgotten what it feels like to set it down.

Mrs. Claus squeezed his arm. "Second thoughts?"

"Third. Fourth. Seventeenth." His voice sounded tired even to himself.

"But you're doing it anyway."

"Have to. Can't let fear make the decisions. Fear never makes good decisions."

She smiled. "That's the man I married."

They walked together toward the office, leaving the workshop to its work, its worry, its hope. Santa's footsteps heavier than usual. Each one requiring just slightly more effort than the last.

Behind them, unseen, Rudolph stood in the stable doorway.

His nose dimmed to almost nothing.

"Good luck, old friend," he whispered. "You're going to need it."

Then he returned to the darkness of the stables, where the other reindeer were arguing about something trivial and Christmas Eve preparations continued and nobody asked him why his nose looked so tired.

Because they all knew.

Being the light everyone points at gets exhausting.

Especially when they keep insisting you're just an LED.

CHAPTER 4
"THE FIRST POST"

~

December 24th, 6:00 AM - North Pole Time

Golden morning light poured through the workshop windows like honey—thick, warm, impossibly perfect. The kind of light that only existed at the North Pole on Christmas Eve morning, when the sun rose at exactly the right angle to make everything look like it belonged in a snow globe.

Santa sat in his chair. His good chair. The one from his office that three young elves had dragged into the workshop because Jinglebert insisted the lighting was "way better in here."

Around him: chaos barely contained as organization.

Jinglebert held a phone—not his tablet, an actual phone, because apparently "mobile content performs 47% better on native devices." He'd said this seventeen times. Santa had stopped asking what it meant.

Young elves hovered at the edges, whispering suggestions:

"Tilt your head a little!" "Smile more!" "No, less! Too much smile looks fake!" "Should we add a filter?" "NO FILTERS!" (That was Jinglebert, horrified.)

Mrs. Claus stood in the doorway, arms crossed, watching with the expression of someone who'd seen this exact scene play out in 1952 with a radio microphone.

"Okay," Jinglebert said, phone raised. "Take... what are we on?"

"Fourteen," an elf supplied.

"Take fourteen! Remember, Santa—natural. Authentic. Just... be yourself!"

Santa looked at the phone. At the little camera lens staring at him like a judgmental eye.

"How do I be myself while being aware of being watched being myself?"

"Just... don't think about it!"

"That's like saying don't think about elephants. Now I'm thinking about elephants."

"Why are you thinking about elephants?!"

"Because you told me not to!"

Several elves giggled.

Jinglebert took a breath. "Okay. Okay. Let's try this. Just... look at the camera. Smile. Say something Christmassy."

Santa looked at the camera.

Tried to smile.

It felt like his face was made of wood.

"Something Christmassy," he said flatly.

"No, don't SAY 'something Christmassy,' say something that IS—"

"Ho ho ho?"

"Too cliché!"

"It's literally my catchphrase!"

"But it sounds PERFORMED!"

"BECAUSE IT IS PERFORMED! YOU'RE MAKING ME PERFORM!"

Mrs. Claus covered her mouth to hide a smile.

"Take fifteen," Jinglebert sighed.

~

TWENTY MINUTES LATER:

They'd tried:

• Santa holding a toy (looked like an advertisement)

• Santa in front of the sleigh (Greta vetoed, security risk)

• Santa with the reindeer (Rudolph refused to participate)

• Santa reading letters (too posed)

• Santa wrapping presents (his hands shook from being watched)

• Santa literally just sitting there (Jinglebert: "You look angry." Santa: "I'M NOT ANGRY." Jinglebert: "...You look angry.")

Take twenty.

Santa slumped in the chair. "I can't do this."

"You can! You're just overthinking!"

"I'm seventeen hundred years old, Jinglebert. Thinking is what I DO."

"But not about THIS! This is supposed to be easy! Natural! Just—"

The workshop door opened.

Mrs. Claus walked in carrying two mugs of cocoa. Steam rose from them like tiny prayers.

She crossed to Santa. Said nothing. Just handed him a mug.

He took it. Wrapped his hands around the warmth. The familiar ceramic. The exact temperature she always got right. His shoulders dropped. The tension in his jaw released.

He looked up at her.

She smiled slightly. Not for the camera. Not for the elves. Just... for him.

That smile that said: I see you. I know you're struggling. You're doing fine.

Santa smiled back. Small. Real. Tired but genuine.

"Thank you," he said quietly.

"THAT!" Jinglebert screamed. "THAT RIGHT THERE!"

Santa jumped. Cocoa sloshed. "What?!"

"THAT was it! That was perfect! The smile! The moment! The AUTHENTICITY!"

"I wasn't ready—"

"EXACTLY!" Jinglebert was practically vibrating. "You weren't performing! You were just... being! That's the one! That's THE ONE!"

He shoved the phone at Santa. On the screen: Santa holding cocoa, looking up at Mrs. Claus (mostly off-frame), smiling that small, real, unguarded smile.

He looked... human. Tired. Real. Like someone's grandfather. Like someone who worked hard and loved what he did and was taking a brief moment to appreciate kindness.

"I look old," Santa said.

"You look REAL," Jinglebert corrected. "You look like Santa. Not the cartoon. Not the mall version. Not the commercial. You look like... you."

Mrs. Claus leaned over Santa's shoulder. Studied the photo.

"Use it," she said.

"Martha—"

"Use it. It's honest. That's what you wanted."

Santa stared at the image. At his own face. At the vulnerability visible in his eyes.

"Alright," he said finally. "Now what?"

"Now we write the caption!" Jinglebert pulled out his tablet (of course he had his tablet). "Okay, I've been working on some options—"

"Let me guess. Sleigh goals?"

"HOW DID YOU—" Jinglebert blinked. "Did Mrs. Claus tell you I was planning that?"

Mrs. Claus smiled innocently.

"Look," Jinglebert continued, "we need something catchy! Engaging! Something that makes people want to interact! Like 'North Pole vibes' or 'Elf szn' or—"

"No."

"But Santa, the algorithm—"

"No."

Santa took the phone. Hunted and pecked with two fingers on the keyboard. Slowly. Deliberately. The way he'd learned to text in 2015 and had never improved.

He typed:

Ready or not, here we come. 🎅 #Christmas2025 #BelieveInMagic

Jinglebert made a small noise of pain. "That's... that's so SIMPLE."

"It's honest."

"But it's not optimized for—"

"It's honest," Santa repeated. "That's the rule."

He looked at the caption. At the photo. At the moment about to become public.

Seventeen hundred years of tradition, contained in one image and thirteen words.

His finger hovered over the POST button.

Shaking.

Just slightly.

Barely noticeable unless you were looking closely.

(Mrs. Claus was looking closely.)

"Santa?" Jinglebert whispered. "You okay?"

"No," Santa said honestly. "But I'm doing it anyway."

Mrs. Claus put her hand on his shoulder. Squeezed gently.

He took a breath.

Tapped POST.

The phone made a small whooshing sound.

The kind of sound that shouldn't mean anything.

The kind of sound that meant everything.

~

30 SECONDS LATER:

"Oh my god."

Jinglebert was staring at his tablet.

"Oh my GOD."

"What?" Santa asked.

"Ten thousand likes. In thirty seconds. TEN THOUSAND."

The young elves gasped.

"That's... good?" Santa ventured.

"That's INSANE! That's—wait, twenty thousand. TWENTY THOU-SAND IN ONE MINUTE."

The elves were crowding around now. Phones out. Pulling up the post on their own devices.

"It's EVERYWHERE!" one elf squealed.

"Look at the shares!"

"The comments are ROLLING!"

"WAIT!" Jinglebert's voice cracked. "ONE HUNDRED THOUSAND! WE'RE AT ONE HUNDRED THOUSAND LIKES IN TWO MINUTES!"

He was crying now. Actually crying. Tears streaming down his face while he hugged his tablet like a child.

"Do you SEE this?" he sobbed at Santa. "Do you SEE?!"

Santa did not see. He was staring at his phone, watching the numbers tick upward so fast they blurred.

234,000 likes.

456,000 likes.

789,000 likes.

"How is this happening?" he asked.

"You're TRENDING!" An elf showed him her phone. "#RealSanta is trending! #NaughtyOrNice is trending! #Christmas2025 is TRENDING!"

"A million," Jinglebert whispered. "We're at a million. In eight minutes. Santa, we're at a MILLION."

"What does that mean?"

"It means EVERYONE is seeing this! It means—WAIT!" Jinglebert zoomed in on something. "WE'RE VERIFIED! We got the blue check-mark! How did we— WHO VERIFIED US?!"

"Maybe Christmas magic?" an elf suggested.

"CHRISTMAS MAGIC DOESN'T WORK ON INSTAGRAM'S SERVERS!"

"Apparently it does!"

The workshop erupted in celebration. Young elves jumping, scream-ing, hugging each other. Jinglebert openly weeping while refreshing metrics. Someone started playing "All I Want for Christmas" and three elves immediately began dancing.

Santa sat in his chair, holding his phone, watching numbers climb.

1.2 million likes.

1.5 million.

2 million.

Trending worldwide.

Featured on the Explore page.

His face—tired, real, holding cocoa—being seen by millions.

And he felt...

Nothing.

No, not nothing.

Empty.

Like eating cotton candy—sweet going in, nothing substantial after.

"Santa?" Mrs. Claus's voice. Quiet. Just for him. "What's wrong?"

"I don't know," he said honestly. "This is what we wanted, right? Engagement? Visibility? Proof we're real?"

"Is it?"

He looked at her. "I know what one letter from one child means, Martha. I know what a family's grateful prayer feels like when it reaches me on Christmas morning. I know what it means when a parent writes 'thank you for seeing us.' But two million... what is two million?"

He stared at the number still climbing on his screen.

"Two million people who don't know my name. Who'll forget this in an hour. Who'll scroll past me like every other thing they see today. Who'll never write a letter or leave cookies or wonder if I'm real in that deep, hopeful way children used to wonder." His voice was quiet. Hollow. "What is two million compared to one child who believes?"

"Two million people who saw you," she said gently.

"Or two million clicks that happened to land on my face."

Around them, the celebration continued. But in their small bubble—Santa in his chair, Martha's hand on his shoulder—there was only quiet uncertainty.

"Maybe check the comments," Mrs. Claus suggested. "See what people are actually saying."

Santa nodded. Scrolled down.

The first comment had 47,000 likes:

fake

The word hit harder than it should have. Harder than any word should hit someone who'd spent seventeen centuries showing up.

The second:

nice try AI

The third:

this is clearly a deepfake

Santa's face went very still.

The phone suddenly felt heavier in his hands. Like it had gained weight with each comment. His chest tightened—not the gentle squeeze from earlier, but something sharper. Colder. The kind of tightness that comes when you realize you've made a terrible mistake and can't take it back.

His breathing changed. Shallower. Faster. Like his body understood before his mind did: this was going to hurt.

He kept scrolling.

bro this is NOT santa 👀

y'all actually believe this?

deepfake detected lmao

His hands—the same hands that had wrapped Walt Disney's first paint set—trembled.

LOL nice costume grandpa

whoever made this has good CGI skills ngl

santa would never use instagram, this is obviously fake

my parents are santa, adults are so dumb 😂

The celebration around him faded into background noise. Distant. Muffled. Like someone had put cotton in his ears.

Mrs. Claus saw his expression. Saw the color draining from his face. "Kris—"

"They think I'm fake," he said quietly.

"Not all of them—"

"Most of them." He kept scrolling. For every supportive comment, there were three calling him AI, deepfake, corporate marketing. "They think this is... what did they call it... engagement bait? Content farming? A publicity stunt?"

"Some do. Not everyone—"

"Jinglebert," Santa said, still staring at the screen.

The young elf stopped mid-celebration. Saw Santa's face. His own smile died.

Jinglebert's ears drooped—something elves did only when the guilt was bone-deep.

"Yes, Santa?"

"How many of these two million people actually believe this is real?"

Jinglebert's face fell. He pulled up analytics. Scrolled. His enthusiasm drained like air from a balloon.

"Um. Based on comment sentiment analysis and... and engagement patterns... maybe 30%? Possibly less?"

"So seven hundred thousand believers," Santa calculated. "And one point three million who think I'm CGI."

The workshop had gone quiet now. Everyone watching Santa. Watching the moment curdle.

The young elves—the ones who'd been jumping and screaming seconds ago—stood frozen. One looked away, couldn't watch Santa's face anymore. Another stared at her phone like it had betrayed her. A third was crying silently, understanding what they'd done.

They'd pushed for this. Begged for it. Promised it would help.

And now they were watching Santa bleed in real-time.

Jinglebert looked stricken. This wasn't what he'd wanted. He'd wanted connection. Belief. Magic spreading. Not... this. Not Santa's face going pale while reading strangers explain away seventeen hundred years of showing up.

"But Santa," Jinglebert tried, his voice breaking slightly, "even if only 30% believe, that's still SEVEN HUNDRED THOUSAND people who—"

"Who will read the comments," Santa finished. "Who will see everyone else calling it fake. Who will second-guess themselves. Who will—"

His phone buzzed.

A new comment, rising to the top:

@SkibidiRizzler: bruh my friend's dad works at a VFX studio, this is literally just rendered footage, y'all are SHEEP 🐑

3,000 likes already.

Santa set the phone down on his lap.

Looked at his hands.

Those hands that had wrapped presents for Marie Curie. Walt Disney. Anne Bradstreet. Generations of children who'd believed without needing proof.

"And so it begins," he said quietly.

Mrs. Claus's hand tightened on his shoulder.

Around them, the young elves had gone silent. The celebration died. Even Jinglebert—still holding his tablet, still watching the metrics climb—looked uncertain now. Looked sick. Looked like he'd just realized what they'd actually done.

Through the window, barely visible in the morning light, Rudolph stood in the stable doorway.

His nose dim.

Almost dark.

Knowing.

Rudolph's silhouette didn't move. Didn't blink. Just watched. Like someone witnessing a prophecy they never wanted to be right about.

I told you, his presence seemed to say. They'll call you fake. And you'll have to carry that.

Santa picked up his phone again. The numbers were still climbing.

2.5 million likes now.

Trending in 47 countries.

Verified checkmark glowing blue.

And comment after comment after comment:

Fake. AI. Deepfake. Nice try. Corporate stunt. LOL. 💀.

"Sir?" Jinglebert's voice was very small. "Do you... do you want me to delete it?"

Santa stared at the screen for a long moment.

Then, slowly, he shook his head.

"No. We post, we own it. This is what we chose."

He stood. Set the phone on the chair. Looked at his team—young and old, celebrating and worried, hopeful and afraid.

"Back to work," he said. "We have presents to load. Reindeer to prep. A flight plan to finalize. Christmas Eve is in twelve hours. The work continues whether they believe or not."

"But Santa—" an elf started.

"The work continues," he repeated. More firmly. "We don't do this for applause. We do this because children need magic. Whether they believe in us or not doesn't change what they need."

He walked toward the door. Paused at the threshold.

"Jinglebert. Keep monitoring. If there's actual useful feedback—not just trolls—let me know. Otherwise, I'll check it tonight. After the deliveries."

"After?" Jinglebert echoed. "But Santa, this is—"

"After," Santa said firmly. "The work comes first. It always has."

He left.

Mrs. Claus followed.

Behind them, the workshop remained frozen. Young elves staring at their phones. Watching the numbers climb. Watching the comments flood. Watching Santa's face spread across the internet while strangers debated whether he was real.

Jinglebert looked at his tablet.

3 million likes now.

Trending in 89 countries.

And the top comment, with 89,000 likes:

this ain't it chief

He set the tablet down.

"Back to work," he said quietly to the others. "You heard Santa. We've got twelve hours until launch."

The elves dispersed. Slowly. Reluctantly. Checking their phones one more time before returning to toy assembly, gift wrapping, sleigh loading.

Only Jinglebert remained in the center of the workshop, staring at the chair where Santa had sat.

Where the morning light had looked so perfect.

Where they'd captured that one real moment.

Where two million people had looked.

And most of them had seen something fake.

"I'm sorry," Jinglebert whispered to the empty room. "I thought this would help."

Outside, the sun continued rising.

Christmas Eve had begun.

And Santa had twelve hours to decide if going viral was worth the cost.

CHAPTER 5
"YOU'RE NOT THE
REAL SANTA"

~

December 24th, 6:15 AM - 10:00 AM

Santa couldn't put the phone down.

It was that simple and that impossible.

He'd returned to his office. Told himself he'd check once more, then get to work. Real work. Loading the sleigh. Reviewing the route. Double-checking the list for last-minute additions.

Real work.

But his thumb kept moving.

Scroll.

Refresh.

Scroll.

The phone glowed in his hands like a cold sun, casting blue light across his face in the dim office. He'd turned off the lamp. Didn't want the warm glow anymore. Just wanted to see the screen clearly.

The numbers kept climbing:

4.2 million likes. 893,000 shares. 47,000 comments.

And counting.

His thumb moved again. Down. Past the supportive comments (there were some, scattered like rare flowers in a field of weeds). Hunting for the ones that hurt.

@CryptoBoySummer: santa would be on Web3 if he was real. this is a scam. probably trying to steal your wallet info.

@MemeLordSupreme: this 'Santa' account is definitely someone's divorced dad trying to go viral. check the Boomer energy in that caption. '#BelieveInMagic' 💀 💀 💀

@TechGirlSarah: I work in AI. This is DEFINITELY generated. Look at the hands around the mug at 0:47—classic rendering artifact.

Santa zoomed in on the photo. Stared at his own hands. They looked fine to him. Real. Weathered. His.

But apparently they had "rendering artifacts."

He refreshed.

New comments loaded:

@SkepticsUnited: everyone in the comments believing this is why misinformation spreads. it's OBVIOUSLY fake. wake up people.

@ConspiracyKevin: SANTA ISN'T REAL WAKE UP SHEEPLE. this is PSYCHOLOGICAL WARFARE to keep you DOCILE and CONSUMING.

@YourMomsBestFriend: nice try fed

Santa didn't know what "fed" meant. Didn't matter. He could feel the hostility through the screen.

Scroll.

Refresh.

Scroll.

@AnimeAvatar2024: my little sister cried when she saw this. she thought Santa was real and now she knows it's just her parents. thanks for ruining Christmas, whoever runs this account.

That one hit different.

A little girl crying.

Because of him.

Because he'd tried to prove he was real and instead proved to some child that he wasn't.

His chest tightened.

Scroll.

Refresh.

Scroll.

His office door opened. He didn't look up.

"Santa?" Jinglebert's voice. Cautious. "We're at 5 million now. That's... that's incredible engagement. The algorithm is really favoring us. We're getting suggested to users who—"

"Read this one," Santa said, not looking up. His voice was flat. Dead. "Kid in Arizona crying because her parents had to admit they were Santa after seeing this post. Says we ruined Christmas."

"That's... that's one comment—"

"This one says I'm a corporate plant trying to sell more toys. This one says I'm a bot. This one says—" His voice cracked slightly. "This one says 'whoever's running this is pathetic. imagine being so desperate for attention you pretend to be Santa.'"

Jinglebert stood in the doorway, tablet hanging limp in his hand.

"Sir, there are supportive comments too—"

"How many?"

"What?"

"How many supportive comments versus negative?"

Jinglebert checked his tablet reluctantly. "About... 35% supportive. 40% skeptical. 25% hostile."

"So two-thirds don't believe," Santa calculated. His thumb kept moving. "Two-thirds think I'm fake. That's 3.3 million people who saw my face and decided I was lying."

"But the 35% who DO believe—"

"Will read the other comments. Will see everyone else saying it's fake. Will doubt themselves." Santa finally looked up. His eyes were red-rimmed. Not from crying. From staring at the screen. "That's how it works, isn't it? One person believes. Ten people say it's fake. The believer starts to wonder."

Jinglebert opened his mouth. Closed it. Had no answer.

Santa's phone buzzed.

New comment, rapidly gaining likes:

@SantaClausReal_Official2: I AM the real Santa. This impostor is stealing MY identity. Check my page for proof. I've been running this account since 2019 with 847 REAL followers.

Santa clicked through.

There he was. The Ohio guy. Profile photo: someone in a Santa suit at what looked like a mall. Bio: "The REAL Santa Claus. Bringing joy to children since 2019. Don't be fooled by imposters. Check verification."

No blue checkmark.

847 followers.

Posts going back years. Hospital visits. Mall appearances. Kids on his lap, genuinely smiling.

And pinned at the top: "BEWARE OF FAKE SANTA ACCOUNTS."

"He thinks I'm the fake," Santa whispered.

"He's just some guy in Ohio," Jinglebert said. "You're the actual—"

"Am I?" Santa looked at his phone. At his verified account with 5.2 million followers. At the Ohio guy's account with 847. "He's been doing this since 2019. Showing up. Visiting kids. No magic, just... showing up. And I'm the one who just appeared yesterday with a verified checkmark and millions of followers. If you didn't know the truth, who would YOU think was real?"

Jinglebert had no answer.

Santa returned to scrolling.

8:00 AM

Mrs. Claus found him in the same position.

Slumped in his chair. Phone glowing. Thumb moving in that awful, compulsive rhythm. His coffee—the one she'd brought at 6:30—sat untouched and cold.

His neck ached from the angle—hunched forward, head tilted down, spine curved in a way it wasn't meant to hold for hours. His eyes burned, dry from not blinking enough, from staring at that cold blue light. His thumb cramped where it touched the screen, the same repetitive motion, scroll-scroll-scroll, until the muscle protested.

"Kris."

No response.

"Kris, put it down."

"They think I'm fake, Martha." His voice was hollow. "After everything. After seventeen hundred years. They think I'm FAKE."

She walked around the desk. Tried to take the phone.

His hand tightened around it. Automatic. Defensive.

"Kris—"

"One more minute. I just need to—"

"You've been saying that for two hours."

He blinked. Looked at her. Really looked. "What?"

"It's eight in the morning. You've been in here since six-fifteen. Staring at that screen. Reading comments. You haven't moved."

"I just need to understand why they—"

"There's nothing to understand. They don't believe. You can't fix that by reading more comments."

But she knew that look in his eyes. Knew it from the radio incident in 1952, when he'd spent three days reading every newspaper article about "Santa's Mistake." Knew it from 2001, when the internet was new and forums were full of people debating whether he was real and he'd found them all.

Kris didn't spiral often.

But when he did, he fell deep.

"Show me," she said gently.

He handed her the phone.

She scrolled. Saw the comments he'd been reading. The ones calling him fake, AI, desperate, pathetic. The little girl crying. The Ohio Santa claiming he was an impostor.

And she saw what Kris had been doing: hearting the negative comments. Not the positive ones. Just the negative.

"Why are you marking these?" she asked.

"So I can find them again. So I can... I don't know. So I can think about how to respond. How to prove—"

"You're hurting yourself," she said quietly. "You're deliberately seeking out pain and holding onto it."

"Someone has to see it. Someone has to—"

"No." She set the phone face-down on the desk. "No, they don't. You posted. They responded. You can't control what they think. You can only control whether you let it destroy you."

He stared at the phone. Face-down. Screen hidden.

His hands shook slightly.

"I can still hear it buzzing," he said.

"I know."

"Every buzz is another comment. Another person seeing me. Another—"

"Another person you can't please."

He looked at her. "That's my job, Martha. Pleasing them. Making them happy. Making them believe."

"Your job is DELIVERING PRESENTS. That's it. That's always been it. You know what they need. You give it to them. Whether they believe or not is their choice."

"But if they don't believe, the magic—"

"The magic works whether they believe or not," she said firmly. "You think every child who got a present believed? You think every parent who found gifts they didn't buy immediately thought 'must be Santa'? No. Some believed. Some didn't. But the presents appeared anyway. The magic happened anyway. Because YOU showed up."

Santa's hands were still shaking.

She took them in hers. Warm palms against his cold fingers.

"You're freezing," she said.

"The phone... it's cold. From the screen."

She held his hands tighter. Warming them.

"Put it away," she said. "Please. Just for a few hours. Get to work. Real work. Load the sleigh. Check the reindeer. Do what you've always done. The comments will still be there tonight if you need to punish yourself by reading them."

He almost smiled at that. Almost.

"What if they're right?" he asked quietly. "What if I AM just... just someone pretending? What if the magic isn't real and I'm just a man who delivers presents and tells himself it matters?"

"Then you're a man who's delivered presents for seventeen hundred years," she said. "And that matters more than any comment section ever could."

She squeezed his hands one more time. Released them. Picked up the phone.

"I'm confiscating this until after the deliveries."

"Martha—"

"After. The. Deliveries." She slipped the phone into her apron pocket.

"You can have it back Christmas morning. When the work is done. When you've remembered what this is actually about."

She left.

The office was suddenly, painfully quiet.

No buzzing. No glowing screen. No comments loading.

Just Santa. His desk. His cold coffee. His shaking hands.

He should feel relieved.

He felt severed.

His hand moved automatically—reached for his pocket where the phone should be. Found nothing. The absence was physical. Like a missing tooth his tongue kept finding. He did it again without thinking. Reached. Found nothing. Reached again.

The phantom weight of it. The phantom glow. The phantom connection to those millions of people who'd seen him and decided he was fake.

Gone.

And he didn't know which was worse: having it and being unable to stop, or not having it and feeling the emptiness where it had been.

9:00 AM - THE WORKSHOP

Santa walked onto the workshop floor in a daze.

The young elves were clustered around a workbench, phones out, squealing.

"Look at this edit someone made!"

"OMG the fanart is already INSANE!"

"Someone made a Spotify playlist called 'Santa's Workout Mix' and it's trending!"

"6.2 MILLION followers now! We gained a million in THREE HOURS!"

Jinglebert was in the center, tablet glowing, practically vibrating with excitement. He saw Santa and rushed over.

"Santa! You won't BELIEVE the analytics! Our engagement rate is 47%—that's INSANE for an account this new! And the shares are—wait, where's your phone?"

"Martha took it."

"She what?"

"Took it. Said I can have it back after the deliveries."

Jinglebert's face fell. "But Santa, we need to capitalize on this momentum! We should be posting stories, engaging with comments, building the narrative! This is prime time for—"

"I can't," Santa said simply. "I was reading comments for two hours. I couldn't stop. It was..." He struggled for the word. "Poisonous."

The young elves had gone quiet. Watching.

"But the metrics—" Jinglebert started.

"I don't care about metrics." Santa's voice was firmer now. "I care about children. And right now, I need to focus on the ones who'll wake up tomorrow morning. Not the ones commenting on Instagram."

He walked past them. Toward the sleigh bay.

Behind him, the young elves exchanged glances.

One whispered: "He doesn't get it."

Another: "He will. Once he sees the impact."

A third: "Did you see the comment about the little girl crying? That was rough."

"Yeah, but it's ONE negative comment in millions of positives!"

"Actually the ratio is more like 65-35 negative to positive if you account for—"

Jinglebert shushed them. "He heard you."

Santa had stopped walking. Stood perfectly still in the middle of the workshop floor.

"What ratio?" he asked without turning around.

Silence.

"Jinglebert. What ratio?"

The young elf clutched his tablet. "Um. Comment sentiment analysis suggests that... roughly 65% of comments are skeptical or negative. And 35% are supportive or neutral."

"And you didn't tell me this."

"I was going to! But you seemed so focused on reading the negative ones yourself and I didn't want to make it worse and—"

Santa turned around slowly.

"So when you said '35% supportive,' what you meant was '65% think I'm fake.'"

"Well... technically... if you break it down by sentiment markers and—"

"Yes or no, Jinglebert."

The elf deflated. "Yes."

Santa nodded slowly. Continued walking toward the sleigh.

Stopped again.

"You're right," he said.

Everyone looked up.

"About what?" Jinglebert asked carefully.

"We need more proof. Better proof. Undeniable proof." Santa turned. His face had changed. Not defeated anymore. Determined. Almost manic. Wild at the edges. "If 65% don't believe, we need to show them something they CAN'T explain away. Something impossible. Something MAGIC."

"Like what?" a young elf asked.

Santa's eyes gleamed with something that looked like desperation wearing a determination mask. "Like the reindeer. Like Rudolph's nose. Like the sleigh flying. Like all of it. Real. Undeniable. On camera."

Jinglebert's eyes widened. "A livestream. You want to do the livestream."

"Not just A livestream. Multiple. The reindeer NOW. The sleigh preparation. The takeoff. The flight tonight. Everything. Every angle. Every moment. Until they have no choice but to believe. Until the evidence is so overwhelming they can't explain it away. Until—"

His voice was rising. Getting faster. The words tumbling out like he was trying to outrun something.

"We'll show them the workshop. The elves making toys. Mrs. Claus baking cookies. The whole operation. Raw footage. Unedited. No tricks. Just reality. They want proof? We'll give them MORE proof than they can process. We'll livestream EVERYTHING until—"

"Santa," an older elf called out—Torbin, who'd been listening from his workbench. "Magic revealed is magic destroyed."

"Magic hidden is magic forgotten!" Santa shot back, and there was something sharp in his voice now. Desperate. "If they don't believe I exist, what good is being mysterious? At least if they SEE the magic, some might—"

"Some might explain it away. Like Rudolph said."

Everyone went quiet.

Rudolph stood in the stable doorway again. His nose dim. His eyes sad.

"You heard?" Santa asked.

"I always hear. Sound carries in barns." The reindeer walked forward slowly. "You want to show them my nose. On camera. To prove it's real."

"Yes."

"And when they call it an LED?"

"They won't be able to. Not when they see it up close. Not when we show them from every angle. Not when we demonstrate the glow patterns, the way it responds to weather, the—"

"Yes, they will." Rudolph's voice was patient. Tired. Kind. "Santa. I love you like a brother. But you're in pain right now. And pain makes bad decisions."

"This isn't pain, this is—"

"You've been reading comments for two hours. Your hands are shaking. You look like you haven't slept. That's pain."

Santa's jaw tightened. "So what do I do? Just... accept that they think I'm fake? Give up?"

"No. Do your job. Load the sleigh. Deliver the presents. BE real, even if they don't believe you're real. That's always been the answer."

"But—"

"There are no buts." Rudolph's voice was gentle but firm. "You can't MAKE them believe, Santa. You never could. Belief is a gift they give you. Not a prize you win."

Santa stood there. Surrounded by elves, old and young. Surrounded by his workshop, his work, his purpose.

And he felt so tired.

The manic energy drained out of him like water from a cracked cup. His shoulders sagged. His eyes lost that wild gleam. What was left looked hollow.

"One livestream," he said quietly. "From the sleigh. Tonight. Just once. To show them I'm doing the work. That I'm real. That's all I'm asking."

Rudolph looked at him for a long moment.

"If that's what you need," he said finally. "But Santa? When they still don't believe—and they won't, not all of them—promise me you'll remember this conversation. Promise me you'll remember that the work is the point. Not the applause."

"I promise."

Rudolph turned back toward the stables. His nose flickered once. Twice.

Then went dark.

10:00 AM

Santa sat on the edge of the sleigh. The workshop bustled around him—elves loading presents, checking manifests, doing the work that always got done no matter what else was happening.

Jinglebert approached carefully.

"Sir? If we're doing the reindeer livestream, we should probably schedule it soon. Give people time to tune in. Build anticipation."

"No reindeer livestream," Santa said quietly.

"What? But you just said—"

"I was wrong. Rudolph was right. We do the delivery livestream only. One brief moment. That's it."

"But the metrics—"

"I don't care about metrics, Jinglebert. I care about..." He trailed off. Looked at his hands. Still shaking slightly from two hours of scrolling. "I care about not becoming something I'm not. Not performing for cameras. Not chasing numbers. Not... not hurting myself trying to convince strangers I exist."

He stood. Looked at the young elf.

"Set up the livestream for tonight. One moment. Brief. General. Nothing specific. Then we turn it off and do the rest in private. Like we always have."

"And if they still don't believe?"

Santa was quiet for a moment.

"Then at least I'll know I tried. And I'll know when to stop trying."

He walked toward the office. Toward his list. Toward the real work.

Behind him, Jinglebert watched him go.

Then looked at his tablet.

7.1 million followers now.

And climbing.

But Santa didn't know that.

And maybe, Jinglebert thought, that was better.

CHAPTER 6
"THE REINDEER INCIDENT"

~

December 24th, 10:30 AM - The Stables

The smell of hay and leather and centuries-old magic filled the air. Reindeer shifted in their stalls, bells jingling softly on their harnesses. Outside, snow fell in that particular North Pole way—straight down, like the sky was sifting sugar.

Santa stood in the center of the stable, surrounded by entirely too many elves with entirely too many cameras.

Jinglebert was setting up three different angles. "Okay, so we'll go live on Instagram, but also simultaneously stream to TikTok and YouTube. Triple the reach!"

"I thought we were doing ONE brief stream," Santa said.

"We are! But we should maximize the platforms while we—"

"One platform. Instagram. That's where we started."

Jinglebert deflated slightly. "Fine. Instagram. But can we at least use the good camera? Phone cameras are great but for something like this—"

"Phone camera. Authentic. That's the rule."

"But—"

"That's. The. Rule."

The young elf sighed. "Okay. Phone camera. Authentic. Got it."

Around them, the reindeer watched with varying levels of interest. Dasher was asleep. Dancer was grooming herself. Prancer was eating hay and judging everyone. Vixen looked annoyed at the disruption. Comet was showing off, pawing the ground and tossing his antlers. Cupid seemed confused about why there were so many elves present. Donner and Blitzen were having a quiet argument about something political.

And Rudolph...

Rudolph stood in his stall at the far end. Separate. Special. The lead reindeer's quarters.

His nose was dark.

Santa walked over slowly. The other sounds faded—the young elves chattering about lighting and angles, Jinglebert testing the audio, someone asking if they should add a filter (immediate chorus of "NO!" from everyone).

"Rudy," Santa said quietly.

The reindeer didn't turn around.

"I know you don't want to do this."

"Then don't ask me to," Rudolph said. His voice was tired. So tired.

"They need to see. They need to understand that the magic is real."

"No, YOU need them to see. I'm fine being doubted. I've been doubted my whole life. I'm used to it."

Santa flinched slightly. That hurt.

Rudolph finally turned around. His nose was still dark, but his eyes... his eyes held something that looked like pity.

"You want to know why I keep my nose dim most of the time?" Rudolph asked.

"Why?"

"Because every time it glows, someone films it. Posts it. And I read the comments. 'Fake.' 'LED.' 'Special effects.' And each time, it hurts a little less. Not because I've gotten stronger. Because I've gotten number."

"Numb," Santa corrected softly.

"Number. Numb. Same thing. The point is—" Rudolph walked closer, until his massive head was level with Santa's face. "—once you show them something magical and they explain it away, you can't unexplain it. That explanation lives in their head forever. 'Santa's reindeer? Oh, I saw a video. Looked fake. LED nose, obvious CGI.' You give them ammunition to doubt you."

"But what if—"

"There is no 'what if.'" Rudolph's voice was gentle but firm. "This is what WILL happen: You'll show them my nose. Three million people will watch. Two million will immediately say it's fake. Half a million will write technical explanations about LED implants or special effects or whatever. The remaining half million will want to believe but will read everyone else's comments and think 'maybe they're right.' And you'll feel worse than you do now."

Santa was quiet.

"But you're going to do it anyway," Rudolph continued. "Because you're in pain and you think proof will stop the pain. So fine. I'll do it. Because I love you. Because you're my friend. Because after seventy-three years of flying together, I owe you that much."

"Rudy—"

"But Santa?" The reindeer's nose flickered. Just once. "When this goes wrong—and it will—remember I told you so. Not because I want to be right. But because someone has to prepare you for what's coming."

He walked past Santa. Toward the center of the stable. Where the cameras waited. Where Jinglebert was bouncing excitedly. Where three million strangers were about to judge whether his magic was real.

His nose began to glow.

Soft at first. Then brighter. Then that brilliant, impossible red that had guided the sleigh through storms and fog and impossible nights for seven decades.

The young elves gasped. Even having seen it a thousand times, Rudolph's nose still took your breath away. It wasn't like a lightbulb. It was like... like captured starlight. Like the feeling of Christmas morning made visible. Like hope given form.

It was beautiful.

"Okay!" Jinglebert called out, positioning his phone. "Everyone ready? We're going live in three... two... one..."

THE LIVESTREAM

The view counter climbed instantly:

327 watching... 1,842 watching... 12,493 watching... 89,347 watching...

Within thirty seconds: 500,000 people watching.

One minute: 1.2 million.

Two minutes: 2.8 million.

Santa stood beside Rudolph, one hand on the reindeer's flank. Trying to look natural. Trying not to perform.

"This is Rudolph," he said to the camera. To the phone. To the 2.8 million strangers. "He's been leading my sleigh for seventy-three years. His nose—well, you can see his nose. It's real. It's not an LED. It's not special effects. It's just... him. This is who he is."

Rudolph's nose glowed steady and red.

The view counter hit 3 million.

Comments began loading:

that's an LED

obvious LED implant

you can literally see the battery pack in his collar

Amazon sells these for $12.99

this is the worst CGI I've ever seen

the lighting is SO fake

whoever edited this needs to learn about shadows

Santa kept talking. Tried to ignore the comments scrolling past. But they were RIGHT THERE. On the screen. Visible. Undeniable.

"His nose isn't powered by batteries. It's just... it's magic. Real magic. It's always been real."

His voice sounded hollow even to himself. The smile he'd put on at the start—the warm, Santa smile—was cracking at the edges. Faltering. Becoming something that looked more like a grimace.

bro that's LITERALLY an LED

you can see where it's attached to his face

this is embarrassing

why are y'all believing this? it's so obviously fake

I can see the WIRES

(There were no wires.)

"Touch it," someone suggested off-camera. "Show them you can touch it!"

Santa hesitated. Then reached up. Put his hand near Rudolph's nose. The red glow illuminated his palm. Warm. Real. Magical.

His hand was shaking. Just slightly. The camera caught it. Three million people saw it.

CGI hand

the glow is POST-PRODUCTION

this is worse than that time they tried to make Sonic look real

nice try Santa's social media team

whoever's running this account is DESPERATE

the hand shake is a nice touch, makes it look more "real" lol

Three and a half million people watching now.

Santa could see the comments. Couldn't stop seeing them. They loaded faster than he could read but he caught phrases:

"pathetic" "obvious fake" "LED" "batteries" "wires" "CGI" "desperate" "sad"

His hand was still near Rudolph's nose. The camera was still rolling. The whole world was watching.

And none of them believed.

He could feel it. The collective disbelief. Three and a half million people looking at real magic and seeing special effects.

"That's all," Santa said abruptly. "Thank you for watching."

"Wait!" Jinglebert hissed. "We're at 3.7 million! Don't end it now!"

But Santa had already turned away.

Jinglebert kept the camera running. Pointed at Rudolph. The reindeer stood there, nose glowing, surrounded by hay and bells and the ancient smell of stable magic.

The comments continued:

poor reindeer probably hates having that LED strapped to his face

this is animal cruelty tbh

PETA should investigate

the reindeer looks uncomfortable

this is sad. whoever's doing this is SAD.

Rudolph's nose flickered.

Then flickered again.

The glow pulsed—once, twice, three times—like a heartbeat slowing down. Like something dying.

Then it dimmed.

Not gradually. Not a gentle fade.

It went dark all at once. Like a switch flipped. Like a choice made.

Rudolph was choosing to hide. Choosing to take his magic back from their cameras, their comments, their explanations. Choosing darkness over display.

He turned. Walked back to his stall. Each step deliberate. Dignified.

Not looking at the camera.

Not looking at anyone.

Jinglebert finally ended the stream.

4.1 million people had watched.

The silence in the stable was deafening.

THE AFTERMATH

Santa stood frozen in the center of the stable. The young elves were already pulling up their phones, checking metrics, reading comments.

"4.1 million viewers!"

"That's INSANE engagement!"

"The clip is already being shared!"

"We're trending again!"

"Look at this meme someone already made!"

One elf—Snowflake, the one with five million Instagram followers—stopped mid-celebration. She was looking at Rudolph's stall. At the darkness where his nose should be glowing.

Her phone lowered slowly.

"Guys," she said quietly.

No one heard her.

"Look at this edit someone made with dramatic music!"

"It's already got 200,000 views!"

"We should do ANOTHER stream! Strike while the iron's hot!"

"Guys," Snowflake said again, louder this time.

Still nothing.

She looked at Rudolph's shadow in his stall. Then at Santa's face. Then at her fellow young elves, celebrating metrics while something precious had just broken.

Her phone went into her pocket.

She didn't take it out again.

Santa walked to Rudolph's stall.

The reindeer stood in shadow. His nose completely dark now.

"Rudy—"

"Don't."

"I'm sorry. I shouldn't have—"

"No, you shouldn't have." Rudolph's voice was quiet. Not angry. Just... done. "But you did. And now four million people think my nose is an LED. They think the magic that's kept me alive for ninety-three years is something you can buy on Amazon for twelve dollars and ninety-nine cents."

"They're wrong—"

"I know they're wrong. YOU know they're wrong. But they don't know. And they won't ever know. Because you gave them an explanation that makes sense to them. LEDs exist. They've seen LEDs. So my nose must be an LED. Simple. Logical. Wrong, but logical."

Santa reached toward him. "Rudy, I'm so sorry—"

"I told you this would happen," Rudolph said. "I TOLD you. And you did it anyway. Because you needed proof more than you needed to protect me."

That landed like a punch.

"That's not—"

"Yes, it is." Rudolph finally turned around. His eyes were sad. Ancient. Tired. "You put me on display. Let them mock me. Let them explain away who I am. Because YOU needed validation."

"I was trying to help!"

"No. You were trying to stop hurting. And you made ME hurt to do it."

The words went through Santa like a blade. Cold. Precise. True.

His throat closed. His chest collapsed inward—not metaphorically, physically, like his ribs were suddenly too small for his lungs. His hands went numb at his sides.

He'd hurt Rudolph. His friend. His partner of seventy-three years. The reindeer who'd never once failed him, never once doubted him, never once asked for anything but to be trusted.

And he'd put him on display for strangers who called his magic fake.

Santa opened his mouth. Closed it. Had nothing to say.

Because Rudolph was right.

Behind them, young elves were still celebrating. Still checking metrics. Still riding the high of 4.1 million views.

"Sir?" Jinglebert called. "The video is BLOWING UP! It's already at 8 million views on TikTok! People are stitching it, duetting it, making reaction videos! This is HUGE!"

Santa didn't turn around.

"Pack it up," he said quietly.

"What?"

"The cameras. The phones. All of it. Pack it up."

"But Santa, we should capitalize on this momentum! We could do another stream! Maybe show the workshop or the sleigh or—"

"NO." Santa's voice was sharp. Final. "No more streams. No more cameras. No more... performance."

He looked at Rudolph.

"You were right," he said softly. "I'm sorry."

Rudolph said nothing. Just turned back around. Facing the wall of his stall.

His nose stayed dark.

Santa walked out of the stables.

The young elves exchanged confused glances.

"But... we got 4.1 million viewers," someone said.

"And eight million views on the viral clip," another added.

"That's SUCCESS! That's what we WANTED!"

Jinglebert looked at Rudolph's dark stall. At Santa disappearing through the door. At Snowflake standing apart from the others, phone still in her pocket, looking stricken.

"I don't think it is," he said quietly.

11:00 AM - SANTA'S OFFICE

Mrs. Claus found him sitting in his chair. Not at his desk. Just... sitting. Staring at nothing.

"I heard," she said.

"Four million people think Rudolph's nose is an LED."

"I know."

"They called it animal cruelty. Said PETA should investigate. Turned his magic into a... a political statement about fake animals being exploited."

"I saw."

"He warned me. He TOLD me this would happen. And I did it anyway."

Mrs. Claus sat on the edge of his desk. "Why?"

"Because I..." Santa's voice cracked. "Because I needed them to believe. I needed to stop feeling like a fraud. I needed..."

"Validation."

"Yes."

"And did you get it?"

He laughed. It sounded like crying. "No. I got four million people explaining away magic. And I hurt my best friend to do it."

She was quiet for a moment.

"Do you know what I did in 1952?" she asked. "After the radio disaster?"

"No."

"I baked. For three days straight. Hundreds of cookies. Thousands. Until my hands cramped and I couldn't stand and the kitchen was full of more cookies than we could possibly need."

"Why?"

"Because I needed to DO something. Something I was good at. Something that didn't require anyone's approval or belief. Something that was real whether anyone was watching or not."

She slid off the desk. Walked to him. Put her hands on his shoulders.

"Go to the workshop. Make toys. Check the list. Load the sleigh. Do the work that matters. Stop trying to prove yourself to strangers who've already decided not to believe."

"But—"

"The delivery is in seven hours. You have seven hours to remember who you are and why you do this. Don't waste them reading comments or planning the next desperate attempt at proof."

She kissed the top of his head.

"Do your job, Kris. Be Santa. Not because they believe. Because children need presents. That's always been enough. Let it be enough again."

She left.

Santa sat alone.

Outside, he could hear the workshop. The sounds of creation. Of purpose. Of work that mattered whether anyone was watching or not.

Slowly, he stood.

Walked to his desk.

Opened the ledger.

And began to work.

Not for validation.

Not for proof.

Not for four million viewers.

For the children who would wake up tomorrow morning.

For the families who needed magic.

For the work itself.

The way it had always been.

The way, maybe, it needed to be again.

CHAPTER 7
"THE DATABASE THREAT"

~

December 24th, 11:45 AM - The Operations Center

The Operations Center was a room most elves never saw.

It sat beneath the workshop, accessible only by a spiral staircase that had been carved from ice in 1823 and somehow never melted. The walls were lined with servers—modern ones, because even magic had to interface with reality sometimes—but also older systems. Punch cards from the 1960s. Ledgers going back centuries. A filing system that predated the Dewey Decimal System and made significantly more sense.

This was where The List lived.

Not the paper version Santa kept in his office. The REAL list. The master database. Every child's name. Every act of kindness. Every small moment of grace or cruelty. Every wish. Every need. Every prayer whispered into the dark hoping someone was listening.

1.8 billion names.

Growing every second.

All maintained by one elf.

Ping.

He was 347 years old. Had been maintaining The List since 1683, when it was still just leather-bound books and his only job was making sure Santa's handwriting stayed legible. He'd watched it evolve through card catalogs, microfiche, early computers, cloud storage, and now this—a hybrid system that was part magic, part technology, and entirely his responsibility.

His workstation had seventeen monitors. Each one showed different data streams:

Real-time updates from global observers (the network of helpers who noticed kind acts). Predictive algorithms (not for determining naughty/nice, but for anticipating needs). Cross-reference systems (connecting families, siblings, friends). The Nice List (glowing gold). The Naughty List (which was actually quite small—children were mostly good). The Needs Analysis (what children required versus what they wanted). And the Security Monitor.

Which was currently screaming.

"No no no no no," Ping muttered, fingers flying across keyboards. Three of them. Simultaneously. He'd learned to type on multiple systems at once in 1997 during the Y2K scare. "Not today. NOT today. Any day but today."

The security monitor flashed red:

UNAUTHORIZED ACCESS ATTEMPT

LOCATION: DISTRIBUTED (BOTNET)

TARGET: NICE/NAUGHTY ALGORITHM

INTENT: DATA EXTRACTION

THREAT LEVEL: CRITICAL

Someone was trying to hack The List.

Not to change it—the magic prevented that. You couldn't just add yourself to the Nice List or remove yourself from the Naughty one. The List knew. It always knew.

No, this was worse.

Someone was trying to expose it.

To download the algorithm. To show the world how Santa "really" decided who was naughty or nice. To prove it was all just... math. Data collection. An invasive surveillance system dressed up as magic.

"No," Ping whispered. His hands were shaking. "You can't. You can't take this. This is forty years. This is my LIFE."

Another alert:

FIRST FIREWALL BREACHED

ESTIMATE: 12 MINUTES TO CORE ACCESS

Twelve minutes until whoever was doing this reached the actual algorithm. The code. The system. The thing that made The List work.

Twelve minutes until magic became mathematics.

His chest felt tight. Not the good tight of excitement—the bad tight of panic. His breathing came faster, shallower. Sweat beaded on his forehead despite the cool underground air. His fingers cramped from typing but he couldn't stop, wouldn't stop, because forty years of work was slipping through his defenses like water through a sieve.

Ping slammed a button. Emergency broadcast.

Throughout the compound, speakers crackled to life:

"CODE CRIMSON. REPEAT. CODE CRIMSON. DATABASE

BREACH IN PROGRESS. ALL SENIOR STAFF TO OPERATIONS CENTER. THIS IS NOT A DRILL."

His voice was shaking.

Forty years of work.

About to be stolen.

About to be explained.

～

11:47 AM

Santa burst through the door first, Mrs. Claus right behind him. Then Jinglebert with his tablet. Torbin, covered in sawdust. Greta, smelling like hay. A dozen other senior elves.

They crowded around Ping's workstation, staring at the screens.

"Talk to me," Santa said.

"Someone's trying to hack The List." Ping's voice was steady but his hands weren't. They danced across keyboards, building countermeasures, raising defenses. "Not to change it. To expose it. To download the algorithm and publish it."

"Who?"

"I don't know. The attack is distributed—routing through thousands of compromised computers worldwide. Could be a hacker collective. Could be a single person with resources. Could be—" He pulled up a trace route. "—oh god."

"What?"

"The attack is sophisticated. Professional. This isn't some kid in a basement. This is... this is someone who knows what they're looking for."

SECOND FIREWALL BREACHED

ESTIMATE: 8 MINUTES TO CORE ACCESS

"Can you stop it?" Mrs. Claus asked.

"I'm trying! I'm building additional encryption layers, randomizing the access paths, fragmenting the data, but—" Ping's voice cracked. "—but they're GOOD. They're really good. They're adapting to every defense I put up."

"What happens if they get in?" Jinglebert asked.

Ping was quiet for a moment.

"They download the algorithm. They see exactly how The List works. Every variable. Every weight assigned to different actions. Every prediction model. Every—" His voice broke completely. "—every piece of magic becomes data. Every mystery becomes code. Every belief becomes skepticism."

"That's not—" Santa started.

"YES IT IS!" Ping spun around in his chair. His eyes were wild. Terrified. "You don't understand! Once they see how it works, once they can EXPLAIN it, it stops being magic! It becomes surveillance! It becomes Big Brother! It becomes 'Santa is watching' in the creepiest way possible! Every parent who ever told their kid 'Santa knows if you've been bad' becomes... becomes evidence of a massive global monitoring system!"

He turned back to the screens. Typed faster.

"They'll call it dystopian. They'll call it invasive. They'll call it a violation of privacy. And they'll be RIGHT, because once you strip away the magic and the belief and the MEANING, all you have left is data collection. And nobody trusts data collection anymore."

THIRD FIREWALL BREACHED

ESTIMATE: 5 MINUTES TO CORE ACCESS

"Shut it down," Torbin said.

Everyone turned.

"What?" Ping asked.

"Shut down The List. Disconnect it. Air-gap the system. If they can't reach it, they can't steal it."

"I can't shut it down! It's Christmas EVE! We need The List to—"

"To what? Deliver presents? Santa's been doing that for seventeen hundred years. He knows what children need. He doesn't need a database to tell him."

"But the efficiency! The optimization! The cross-referencing! Without The List, we're—"

"We're doing it the old way," Torbin said firmly. "Paper. Memory. Instinct. The way it was done before computers."

"That's INSANE!" Jinglebert protested. "There are 1.8 BILLION children! You can't manage that with PAPER!"

"We managed it before."

"When there were TEN MILLION children! The population has exploded! The complexity has—"

FOURTH FIREWALL BREACHED

ESTIMATE: 3 MINUTES TO CORE ACCESS

"STOP ARGUING!" Ping screamed. "I'm losing this! I'm LOSING!"

His hands flew across keyboards. But for every defense he raised, the attack adapted. It was like fighting smoke. Like trying to hold water. The hacker—whoever they were—was too good.

Too smart.

Too determined.

"Why?" Ping whispered. "Why would someone do this? Why would someone want to destroy belief? What do they gain?"

On one of the monitors, a message appeared.

Not from the system.

From the hacker.

You want to know why?

Because you're lying to children. Because "Santa sees you when you're sleeping" is SURVEILLANCE. Because the world deserves to know that magic is just algorithms and data collection. Because TRUTH matters more than belief.

Because I was a kid once who believed, and when I found out the truth, I felt BETRAYED. So I'm returning the favor.

I'm exposing you. All of you.

And there's nothing you can do to stop me.

- J.M.

The room went silent.

"J.M.," Santa said quietly.

"Mean anything to you?" Greta asked.

"No. But they're not wrong. Not entirely." Santa stared at the message. At the anger visible in every word. "We DO watch. We DO collect data. We DO maintain lists of who's been good and who hasn't. The only difference between us and the surveillance state is intent. We do it with love. They think we do it with control."

"That's a BIG difference," Mrs. Claus said.

"Is it? If we can't explain the difference? If all they see is the mechanism without the meaning?"

FINAL FIREWALL UNDER ATTACK

ESTIMATE: 90 SECONDS TO CORE ACCESS

"SOMEONE DECIDE!" Ping yelled. "Shut it down or let me keep fighting! But DECIDE!"

Everyone looked at Santa.

He stood there, surrounded by screens showing a lifetime of work about to be stolen. Surrounded by elves waiting for him to choose. Surrounded by the weight of seventeen hundred years of tradition hanging in the balance.

And he thought about the last four hours.

The Instagram post that went viral while strangers called him fake.

The livestream where four million people watched Rudolph and decided his magic was an LED.

The comments. The mockery. The explanations.

The constant, exhausting need to prove himself real.

And now this.

Someone trying to expose the machinery behind the magic.

To prove that Santa Claus was just data collection and algorithms.

To show that belief was misplaced and magic was mathematics.

They weren't entirely wrong.

"What matters more?" Mrs. Claus asked quietly. Just for him. "That they believe in you? Or that the presents appear?"

Santa looked at her.

"The presents," he said.

"Then what do we do?"

He turned to Ping. To the elf who'd given forty years to maintaining The List. Who'd adapted to every change. Who'd kept the system running through Y2K and 9/11 and every crisis that had threatened to expose or destroy Christmas.

Santa took a breath.

The room waited.

Ping's hands hovered over the keyboards, ready to fight, ready to defend, ready to keep trying even though he was losing.

And Santa said two words that changed everything:

"Let it go."

The words fell into the Operations Center like stones into still water.

Silence.

Complete, shocked, disbelieving silence.

"WHAT?!" Ping's voice cracked.

"Let them take it. Stop fighting."

"But forty years of work! Forty years of—"

"Is going to be stolen either way," Santa said gently. "You're fighting brilliantly. But you're losing. And in—" he checked the monitor, "—seventy seconds, they'll have it anyway. So let it go. Save your energy. We have deliveries to make."

"But—"

"Ping." Santa walked over. Put his hand on the elf's shoulder. "You've done amazing work. This system is beautiful. But it's not more important than the actual delivery. They want to expose the algorithm? Fine. Let them. Let the whole world see how we track kindness and need. Let them debate whether it's surveillance or service. While they're arguing about data, we'll be delivering presents."

60 SECONDS TO CORE ACCESS

Ping stared at Santa. At the hand on his shoulder. At the man who'd just given permission to let forty years of work be stolen.

The room remained frozen. Torbin's mouth slightly open. Greta's eyes wide. Jinglebert clutching his tablet like it might fly away. Young elves looking at each other, uncertain, afraid.

No one had expected this.

Everyone had expected Santa to fight. To rage. To demand they find a way to stop it.

But instead: "Let it go."

"You're sure?" Ping whispered.

"I'm sure. Stop fighting. Let them take it. And then we do our jobs anyway."

Slowly—so slowly it looked like it hurt—Ping's hands lifted from the keyboards.

His fingers twitched. Muscle memory wanting to keep typing. Wanting to keep fighting. Wanting to save what he'd built.

But he pulled his hands back. Folded them in his lap.

And surrendered.

The screens continued their countdown.

30 SECONDS

Around them, elves watched in stunned silence. Watching forty years of work slip away. Watching Santa choose... what? Giving up? Or something else?

15 SECONDS

Mrs. Claus squeezed Santa's arm.

10 SECONDS

Ping closed his eyes. His lips moved—maybe a prayer, maybe a goodbye to the system he'd loved.

5 SECONDS

The room held its breath.

ACCESS GRANTED

The security monitor flashed green.

Then red.

Then displayed a new message:

DOWNLOAD INITIATED

FILES EXTRACTED: NICE/NAUGHTY ALGORITHM

PREDICTION MODELS: ACQUIRED

HISTORICAL DATA: SECURED

UPLOAD DESTINATION: WIKILEAKS + MULTIPLE NEWS OUTLETS

ESTIMATED TIME TO PUBLICATION: 4 HOURS

The words glowed on the screen. Stark. Final. Done.

Forty years of work, extracted in seconds.

Ping's shoulders shook. Not sobbing—not yet—just the physical response to loss. His breath came in short, sharp gasps. His hands, now useless in his lap, trembled.

Around the room, elves stared at the screen in horror. At the magnitude of what had just been stolen. At the implications spreading through their minds like cracks in ice.

This wasn't just data.

This was proof.

Proof that magic was mathematics.

Proof that Santa was surveillance.

Proof that belief was based on lies.

Below that, another message from J.M.:

Thank you for making this easy.

The world will know the truth by tonight.

Merry Christmas, "Santa."

Hope the publicity is worth it.

The room was silent.

Forty years of work.

Gone.

About to be published.

About to be analyzed.

About to be explained, dissected, criticized, and turned into ammunition against belief.

Ping made a sound. Not quite a sob. Not quite a scream. Something in between.

"I'm sorry," he whispered. "I'm so sorry. I should have—"

"You did everything right," Santa said firmly. "This isn't your fault. They were better. That's all. Sometimes being good isn't enough."

He turned to the room. To his senior staff. To the young elves who'd been celebrating viral videos three hours ago and were now watching their operation get exposed in real-time.

"We have seven hours until launch," Santa said. "In four hours, every news outlet in the world is going to have our algorithm. They're going to analyze it. Critique it. Call it invasive or dystopian or whatever they decide it is. And we can't stop that. We can't control what they think. We can only control what we DO."

He walked to the center of the room.

"So here's what we do: We prep the sleigh. We load the presents. We check the harnesses. We review the route. We do every single thing we'd do on any other Christmas Eve. And at midnight, we launch. And we deliver presents to 1.8 billion children. Not because they believe in us. Not because anyone's watching. Not because the algorithm told us to."

He paused.

"We do it because it's our JOB. We do it because those children wake up tomorrow needing to know someone cares. We do it because magic isn't in the algorithm—it's in the SHOWING UP."

He looked at each of them.

"Four hours from now, they'll know how we track kindness. They'll see our prediction models. They'll read our code. And they'll explain away the magic with mathematics. Fine. Let them. While they're writing think-pieces about surveillance and data ethics, we'll be doing the actual work of Christmas."

Torbin smiled. Just slightly. "Now THAT sounds like the Santa I know."

"But sir," Jinglebert said quietly, "what about the backlash? What about when parents see that we've been tracking their children's behavior? What about the privacy concerns? What about—"

"What about them?" Mrs. Claus interjected. Her voice was steel wrapped in silk. "Let them be concerned. Let them debate. Let them protest. None of that changes what needs to happen tonight. Children need presents. We deliver presents. Everything else is noise."

She looked at Santa. A whole conversation in that look.

Are you ready to let go?

Are you ready to stop fighting for belief?

Are you ready to just DO THE WORK?

Santa nodded slightly.

"Ping," he said. "Log everything. Document what happened. When they publish, we'll have our own record. We won't hide. We won't deny. We'll just... explain. Honestly. 'Yes, we track kindness. Yes, we notice who needs help. Yes, we maintain lists. Because we care. Because someone has to see the children everyone else overlooks.'"

Ping nodded slowly. Hands already moving to create the documentation.

"Torbin, Greta—final sleigh inspection. I want every bolt checked, every harness tested. If we're going to do this under scrutiny, we do it PERFECTLY."

They nodded. Left.

"Jinglebert—"

The young elf looked up, tablet clutched to his chest like a shield.

"—no more social media until after the deliveries. I want you in the workshop. Actually WORKING. Making sure the last batch of toys is perfect. Can you do that?"

Jinglebert looked at his tablet. At the metrics. At the comments section he'd been compulsively checking.

Then he set it down on the desk.

"Yes, sir. I can do that."

"Good. Everyone else—to your stations. We launch in seven hours. Let's make sure we're ready."

The room emptied. Elves heading to their posts. To the work. To the purpose that existed whether anyone believed or not.

Only Mrs. Claus and Santa remained.

And Ping, still at his workstation, watching the download complete.

"I built something beautiful," Ping said softly. "I built a system that helped us see every child. Every need. Every moment of grace. And in four hours, it's going to be called surveillance. It's going to be called invasive. It's going to be turned into the villain."

"I know," Santa said.

"Does that bother you?"

Santa was quiet for a long moment.

"Yes," he admitted. "It bothers me that good work will be misunderstood. It bothers me that we'll be villainized for caring. It bothers me that they'll see the data without seeing the love."

He walked to the door. Stopped at the threshold.

"But it bothers me more that I almost forgot what matters. That I almost let the need to be believed become more important than the work itself. That I almost sacrificed everything—including Rudolph's dignity—for strangers' approval."

He looked back at Ping.

"Your work is beautiful. The algorithm is brilliant. And when they publish it, some people will see that. They'll see how much thought went into making sure every child is seen. They'll understand that this isn't surveillance—it's love made systematic."

"And the ones who don't understand?" Ping asked.

"We deliver their children's presents anyway," Santa said simply.

He left.

Mrs. Claus lingered a moment longer.

"You did good work, Ping," she said gently. "Forty years of beautiful, complicated, caring work. And no matter what they say about it in four hours, I hope you remember: this system helped us see children who would have been overlooked. That's not surveillance. That's grace."

She followed Santa out.

Ping sat alone in the Operations Center, surrounded by screens showing code being stolen, work being exposed, magic being explained.

His hands hovered over the keyboard for a long moment.

Then, slowly, deliberately, he began to type.

Not defenses. Not countermeasures. Not desperate attempts to undo what had been done.

Documentation.

He titled the file: "The Truth About The List: A 40-Year Love Letter."

And he wrote.

About the first time he'd noticed a pattern—a child in Bangladesh who always shared her lunch, whose name kept appearing in positive reports, who deserved to be seen.

About the algorithm that wasn't designed to punish but to notice. To witness. To make sure no act of kindness was too small to matter.

About the nights he'd stayed late, refining the code, not to make it more invasive but to make it more compassionate. To catch the moments everyone else missed.

About the children whose needs the system had identified—not because they'd been bad, but because they'd been invisible. The quiet ones. The ones whose parents couldn't afford much. The ones who gave and gave and never asked for anything back.

His fingers flew across the keyboard now. Not fighting. Not defending.

Just telling the truth.

When they published the algorithm, they'd publish it naked. Raw code stripped of context. Mathematics without meaning.

So he was writing the context. The meaning. The forty years of intention that lived between every line of code.

Not because it would change their minds.

But because if someone—anyone—wanted to understand, they deserved to know the full story.

Not surveillance.

Grace.

Not control.

Witness.

Not Big Brother.

Someone who sees you when you're sleeping because someone should see that you gave your blanket to your little sister when she was cold.

His vision blurred. Whether from tears or exhaustion or forty years of work ending on a stolen Tuesday afternoon, he wasn't sure.

But he kept typing.

Because truth deserved to be told completely.

Even when—especially when—no one was ready to hear it.

12:30 PM - SANTA'S OFFICE

Santa stood at the window, watching snow fall.

Mrs. Claus brought him tea. Set it on his desk. Stood beside him.

"How do you feel?" she asked.

"Lighter," he said. Surprised. "I thought I'd feel worse. But I feel... lighter."

"Because you let go."

"Because I stopped fighting. Stopped trying to control what I can't control. Stopped needing to be believed."

"And what are you going to do instead?"

He smiled. Tired. Real.

"My job. Just... my job. The way I should have been doing all along."

She leaned against him. They stood together, watching snow fall, seven hours before the most scrutinized Christmas Eve in history.

"Do you think they'll understand?" she asked. "When they see the algorithm?"

"No," Santa said honestly. "Most won't. They'll see surveillance without seeing the care. Data without seeing the love. Algorithms without seeing the intention."

"Does that bother you?"

"Yes. But not as much as it bothers me that I almost lost myself trying to convince them otherwise."

He turned from the window. Walked to his desk. Opened the ledger.

"Seven hours until launch," he said. "I have names to review. Needs to notice. Work to do."

"And the hack? The exposure?"

"Happens whether I worry about it or not. So I choose not to worry. I choose to do what I can do. Which is this." He gestured to the ledger. "The actual work."

Mrs. Claus smiled.

"There you are," she said softly. "There's my Kris."

He looked up. "Where was I before?"

"Lost. Chasing validation. Hurting people to prove yourself. But you're back now. And that's what matters."

She kissed his forehead. Left him to his work.

Santa sat at his desk. Picked up his pen. Opened the ledger to the next name.

Timothy Henderson, age 7. Needs his parents to remember why they fell in love.

Sarah Martinez, age 34. Needs to know she's doing a good job.

Kevin Patterson, age 42. Needs to know someone sees his grief.

One name at a time.

One need at a time.

One present at a time.

The way it had always been.

The way it needed to be again.

Outside, the countdown continued:

3 HOURS 28 MINUTES UNTIL ALGORITHM PUBLICATION

6 HOURS 58 MINUTES UNTIL LAUNCH

And Santa Claus, who'd spent the morning chasing approval, spent the afternoon doing the only thing that actually mattered:

Seeing people.

Knowing their names.

Preparing to show up.

Whether anyone believed he would or not.

CHAPTER 8
"THE CHIMNEY VIDEO"

~

December 24th, 4:00 PM - Final Proof Attempt

The afternoon light was dying. That particular December twilight where the world turns blue and gold and seems to hold its breath before the dark.

Santa stood in the workshop, holding a GoPro.

It was so small. So light. Barely there.

But it felt like it weighed a thousand pounds.

"You don't have to do this," Mrs. Claus said. She stood in the doorway, arms crossed, watching him with that expression—the one that said she'd support him but wouldn't pretend to agree.

"One more time," Santa said. His voice was quiet. Steady. The voice of a man who'd made a decision and couldn't be talked out of it. "Just once more. Real proof. Undeniable proof."

"Kris—"

"The algorithm gets published in two hours, Martha. TWO HOURS. Every news outlet in the world is going to see our data and call it surveillance. Every parent is going to read think-pieces about how we've been 'spying' on their children. Every—" His voice cracked. "Every bit of good we do is going to be turned into something sinister."

"And you think a video will fix that?"

"I think if they SEE the magic—really see it, undeniably see it—they'll understand we're not the villain. We're just... we're trying to help."

Mrs. Claus walked closer. Put her hand on the GoPro. On his hand holding it.

"What are you really trying to prove?" she asked gently. "That you're real? Or that you're good?"

Santa looked at her. At those eyes that had seen him at his best and worst for four hundred years.

"Both," he admitted. "I need them to know I'm real. And I need them to know I'm not... not what the algorithm is going to make me look like."

She studied his face for a long moment.

"Then do it," she said finally. "But Kris? When this doesn't work—and it won't—promise me you'll stop. Promise me you'll just do the deliveries and come home. No more proof. No more fighting. Just the work."

"If this doesn't work," Santa said, and his voice had that edge of desperation, that brittleness of someone holding on by fingernails, "then I don't know what else to do."

She kissed his cheek. "Then let's hope it works."

But her eyes said: It won't work. It never does. But you need to see that for yourself.

~

4:15 PM - TEST HOUSE

They picked a house in Colorado. Random. Middle-class. Two kids, both asleep (timezone magic—4 PM North Pole time, 9 PM Colorado time). Parents downstairs watching TV.

Perfect.

Santa positioned the GoPro on his hat. Checked the angle. Jinglebert —operating the sleigh's communication system remotely—gave a thumbs up on the screen.

"Camera's rolling," Jinglebert's voice came through the earpiece. "Streaming directly to a secure server. We'll post it after you're done. Can't risk live interference."

"Got it."

Santa stood on the roof. The chimney loomed before him—red brick, standard diameter, impossible for a man of his size to fit through.

But he'd been doing impossible things for seventeen hundred years.

He looked at the camera. Tried to smile. It felt like his face was cracking.

"This is real," he said to the lens. To the future viewers. To the doubters. "All of it. What you're about to see is real magic. No tricks. No wires. No special effects. Just... me. Doing what I've always done."

He stepped toward the chimney.

The magic happened.

~

THE FOOTAGE

The GoPro captured everything in perfect high-definition:

Santa's boots touching the chimney edge.

The slight shimmer in the air—like heat waves, but cold. The visual distortion of magic working.

His body compressing. Not shrinking exactly. Just... fitting. Folding into dimensions that shouldn't exist. Shoulders narrowing. Height reducing. Mass redistributing in ways that violated every law of physics.

The descent.

Brick walls rushing past. The camera bounced slightly—human movement, not computer-generated smoothness. The darkness of the chimney. The sound of fabric against brick. His breathing.

Then: the fireplace opening.

Emerging into the living room.

The Christmas tree in the corner, lights twinkling. The stockings hung on the mantle. The cookie plate (three cookies, one already half-eaten by a kid who couldn't wait).

Santa's full size restored. The magic reversing. Physics reasserting itself in reverse.

He moved quietly. Pulled presents from the bag (bigger on the inside —another impossible thing). Placed them under the tree. Ate a cookie (chocolate chip, homemade, still slightly warm). Drank the milk.

Then—and he did this without thinking, just instinct—he looked at the camera. Gave a little wave. A small smile. Genuine.

Hi. I'm here. I'm real. This is real.

Back up the chimney. The compression happening again. The magic visible. Undeniable.

The camera captured it all.

Perfect. Clear. Impossible to explain away.

Right?

~

4:45 PM - THE POSTING

They uploaded it to Instagram.

No fancy caption. Just:

Since you asked for proof. Merry Christmas. 🎅

Posted at 4:47 PM North Pole time.

Within seconds: 10,000 views.

One minute: 100,000 views.

Five minutes: 1 million views.

And the comments started loading.

Santa sat in the sleigh, phone in hand, Mrs. Claus beside him on the comm screen, and watched the response come in.

@AIDetectorPro: This is AI-generated. Sora or similar. Look at the pixel artifacts around the chimney at 0:23. Dead giveaway.

@FilmStudent_Jake: As someone studying VFX, I'm actually impressed by this. The particle effects on the "shrinking" are really well done. Must've taken days to render.

@TechAnalyst_Maria: Pausing at 0:47—you can see where they composited different footage. The lighting doesn't match between the chimney interior and the living room. Classic greenscreen error.

@PhysicsProf_Anderson: Setting aside whether this is "real"—the physics here are fascinating. If this WERE real, Santa would need to exist in at least 4 dimensions to compress like that. Which obviously he doesn't. So: CGI. Well-made CGI, but CGI.

@SkepticsUnited: I teach media literacy and I'm using this as an example in class. Look at the frame rate changes during the "magic" moments. That's post-production editing, not magic.

Santa scrolled. Kept scrolling.

His chest was getting tight again. That familiar pressure. But different this time. Not panic. Not anger. Something worse.

The slow, creeping realization that nothing would ever be enough.

His hands trembled slightly holding the phone. Not from fear. From the effort of holding onto something—hope, maybe—that was slipping away with every comment.

@DeepFakeFinder: Ran this through my detection software. 94% confidence it's AI-generated. The face is probably deepfaked onto a body actor.

@CryptoBoySummer: This is what generative AI can do now. Amazing technology, terrible application. Stop lying to kids.

@GraphicDesigner_Mia: Okay but can we appreciate how GOOD this is? The attention to detail, the lighting, the seamlessness? Whoever made this is talented.

Santa stopped scrolling.

Read that last one again.

"Whoever made this is talented."

The words sat on the screen. Glowing. Innocent. Devastating.

Someone was complimenting the craftsmanship of his actual life.

Someone was reviewing his existence like it was a portfolio piece.

Like he was an artist who'd created something impressive.

Like his seventeen hundred years of showing up, his magic, his PURPOSE—was an art project worthy of praise.

He stared at those words until they stopped making sense. Until they were just shapes. Just pixels. Just another thing that didn't mean what it should mean.

His throat closed. His vision blurred slightly. Not tears—just the body's response to realizing you've been screaming into a void and the void is analyzing your vocal technique.

His breathing came shallow. Quick. The phone felt heavier in his hands. Or maybe his hands felt weaker. He couldn't tell anymore.

He felt something inside him go very quiet. Very still.

Not anger.

Not sadness.

Just... nothing.

The hollow feeling of realizing you're performing your life and someone's grading your technique.

He kept scrolling. His thumb moved automatically now. Compulsively. Like scratching a wound.

@MovieBuffMike: The tracking on the cookie-eating shot is PERFECT. How'd they keep the crumbs so realistic? Practical effects mixed with CGI?

@TechReviewDaily: This is probably made with a combination of Sora AI for the chimney sequence, practical filming for the house interior, and some light post-production. Very seamless work.

@VFXProTom: I work at ILM. This is better than some of our stuff. Whoever made this—we're hiring. DM me.

Santa made a sound. Not quite a laugh. Not quite a sob.

"They want to hire me," he said. His voice was flat. Empty. Like all the emotion had leaked out through some crack he couldn't find. "They think I'm a VFX artist and they want to hire me."

"Kris—" Mrs. Claus started.

"They're analyzing the 'particle effects' on the magic. They're complimenting my 'rendering techniques.' They're offering me a JOB making fake things that look real, because they think I made a fake thing that looks real, except it's NOT FAKE, IT'S JUST MY LIFE."

He was breathing harder now. Not yelling. Worse than yelling. Just stating facts in that terrible, empty voice.

"I went down a chimney. I compressed my body using magic that's kept this job running for seventeen hundred years. I delivered presents to two kids who need to believe someone cares. And they're reviewing it like it's a TECH DEMO."

His hands were shaking now. Visibly. The phone trembling in his grip.

"Sir," Jinglebert's voice came through the comm, careful, "we're at 3 million views now. And... the Pixar comment is getting a lot of engagement."

"Read it," Santa said.

"Santa—"

"Read it."

Jinglebert's voice came through, quiet: "Whoever made this should work for Pixar. The attention to detail is incredible. The way the coat folds during the shrinking, the brick texture, the milk surface tension—everything is perfect. This is what animation should aspire to."

Silence.

Then: "7,000 likes. And climbing."

Santa set the phone down. Very carefully. Like it might explode. Or like he might throw it.

He looked at Mrs. Claus on the comm screen.

"They're aspiring to me," he said. "They're aspiring to replicate what I actually do. They're setting their sights on creating something as 'realistic' as my real life."

Mrs. Claus's face on the screen was heartbroken.

"Kris. Put it down. Please."

"I did everything. EVERYTHING. I showed them the workshop. The reindeer. The magic. I went down a CHIMNEY on CAMERA and they think it's—" His voice broke. "—they think it's impressive technology."

"Kris—"

"What do I have to do, Martha? What do I have to DO to make them believe I'm real?"

She was quiet for a moment.

Then, very gently: "Nothing. Because you can't make them believe. Belief is a choice. You can show them everything—every piece of magic, every impossible thing—and they'll find a way to explain it. Because that's safer than believing. Explaining is easier than faith."

"So I just... give up?"

"No. You do what you've always done. You deliver the presents. You show up. You see the children who need to be seen. Whether anyone believes or not."

"But—"

"Kris." Her voice was firm now. Steel wrapped in love. "Does their disbelief change what those children need?"

He opened his mouth.

Closed it.

"Does it?" she pressed. "Those two kids in that house—do they need presents less because three million people think you're CGI?"

"...No."

"Does Kevin need his photo albums less because people think your algorithm is surveillance?"

"No."

"Does Sarah need to know she's doing a good job less because strangers don't believe you exist?"

"No."

"Then what. Does. It. Matter?"

The question hung in the air.

Santa looked at the phone. At the 3.2 million views. At the comments still loading—half impressed by the "VFX work," half calling it fake, none of them believing it was real.

He'd shown them everything.

Given them undeniable proof.

And they'd denied it anyway.

Because they could.

Because explaining was easier than believing.

Because in 2025, nothing was so magical it couldn't be explained away with technology.

Something was shifting inside him. Not breaking—he'd been breaking all day. This was different. This was pieces settling into a new configuration. A new understanding.

He could keep fighting. Could post more videos. Could give them more proof. Could spend the rest of his existence trying to convince strangers that his life was real.

Or.

He could just live it.

Whether they watched or not. Whether they believed or not. Whether they understood or not.

The work was real. The children were real. The need was real.

That was enough.

That had always been enough.

He'd just forgotten.

"It doesn't matter," he said quietly. "Their belief doesn't matter. Not compared to the work."

"Say it again," Mrs. Claus said.

"Their belief doesn't matter."

"Again. Like you mean it."

"Their belief doesn't matter." Stronger now. Clearer. Like fog lifting. "The work matters. The children matter. Showing up matters. Whether they believe or not—I show up anyway."

Mrs. Claus smiled. Sad but proud.

"There you are," she said softly. "There's my Kris. Took you all day, but there you are."

Santa picked up the phone. Looked at it one more time.

4.1 million views.

12,000 comments.

Trending worldwide.

And not one single person in the top 100 comments believed it was real.

Not one.

He opened Instagram. Navigated to his account. Looked at the three posts:

The photo with cocoa (6.2 million likes). The reindeer livestream (4.9 million views). The chimney video (4.1 million views and climbing).

Fifteen million engagements.

And according to Jinglebert's sentiment analysis: 68% didn't believe.

Ten million people saw his face, his magic, his work.

And seven million decided it was fake.

He typed one more post:

Believe or don't. Either way, the presents will be there in the morning. Merry Christmas. 🎅

Posted it.

Then—and this felt like the most important thing he'd done all day—he held the phone in both hands.

Looked at it. Really looked at it.

This small rectangle of glass and circuitry. This window to millions of strangers who would never know him. This thing that had consumed his entire day, his attention, his peace.

This thing that had made him hurt Rudolph. Made him forget what mattered. Made him perform his life instead of living it.

He thought about keeping it. Just in case. Just to check one more time. Just to see if maybe, possibly, someone had finally believed.

But he knew how that would go. One check would become ten. Ten would become fifty. Fifty would become another day lost to scrolling, to seeking validation, to hoping strangers would finally see him.

No.

He was done.

Santa powered down the phone.

Watched the screen go dark. Watched his reflection disappear from the glass. Watched the connection to those millions of strangers sever.

It felt like setting down a weight he'd been carrying so long he'd forgotten it wasn't part of him.

It felt like exhaling after holding his breath for hours.

It felt like coming home.

He opened the glove box.

Placed the phone inside.

Closed the glove box.

And walked toward the stables.

Where Rudolph waited.

Where an apology was owed.

Where the work continued, whether anyone believed in it or not.

5:30 PM - THE STABLES

Rudolph's stall was dark.

"Rudy?" Santa called softly.

No response.

"I know you're in there. And I know you're angry. You have every right to be. I..." He stopped at the entrance to the stall. "I'm sorry. I'm so, so sorry."

Still nothing.

Santa stepped inside.

Rudolph stood in the corner, facing the wall. His nose completely dark.

"I put you on display this morning," Santa said. "Let strangers mock you. Let them call your magic an LED. Let them hurt you because I needed validation. That was wrong. Deeply, profoundly wrong."

Rudolph's ear flicked. Listening.

"I spent all day trying to prove we're real. Posted videos. Showed the magic. Gave them everything. And you know what they did?"

Silence.

"They explained it away. Every single time. Called it VFX. Called it AI. Called it deepfake. Analyzed it frame by frame. Complimented my 'rendering techniques.' Offered me a job at Pixar."

Rudolph made a sound. Not quite a snort. Almost like... was he laughing?

"You were right," Santa continued. "You told me this would happen and I didn't listen. I hurt you for nothing. Because people determined not to believe will find a way not to believe. No matter what proof you give them."

Rudolph turned around slowly.

His nose was still dark.

But his eyes... his eyes weren't angry anymore.

Just tired.

"I told you," he said quietly.

"You did."

"And you did it anyway."

"I did."

"And you learned."

"I did."

They stood there. Old friends. Partners for seventy-three years. One who'd learned the lesson long ago, one who'd needed to learn it today.

Santa took a step closer. His voice dropped lower. Softer. More honest than he'd been all day.

"I forgot what mattered," he said. "Forgot that the light you give—the literal light from your nose, the figurative light of showing up, of being there—that light doesn't shine because anyone's watching. It shines because that's what it does. That's what YOU do."

Rudolph was very still. Listening.

"And I asked you to make your light about them. About proving. About performing. When your light has never been about any of that." Santa's voice cracked slightly. "Your light is about the work. About guiding. About showing the way through fog and storm and doubt. And I'm sorry I forgot that. I'm sorry I asked you to cheapen it."

Rudolph's eyes—ancient, knowing, kind—studied Santa's face.

"I'm sorry," Santa said again. "For this morning. For the cameras. For using you to try to prove myself. You deserved better."

The silence stretched.

Then Rudolph walked closer. Stood nose-to-nose with Santa.

"You done now?" he asked. "Done trying to convince them?"

"Yeah. I'm done."

"Ready to just do the work?"

"Yeah."

"Good." Rudolph's nose flickered. Just once. "Because we've got 1.8 billion deliveries to make. And I don't care if they think I'm an LED. I've got flying to do."

His nose flared bright.

Not for cameras.

Not for proof.

For the work.

Santa smiled. "Thank you."

"Don't thank me. Just don't put me on TikTok again."

"Deal."

They stood together in the stable. The old team. Ready for the old work.

"Hey Rudy?"

"Yeah?"

"Those people who said you're an Amazon LED for $12.99?"

"Yeah?"

"They have no idea what they're talking about. Your nose is worth at least twenty dollars."

Rudolph snorted. Actual laughter this time.

"Get out of my stable and go finish prep," he said. "We launch in four and a half hours."

"Yes, sir."

Santa walked toward the door. Stopped at the threshold.

"Rudy?"

"Yeah?"

"I'm glad you're my friend."

"Me too, old man. Me too."

Santa left.

Behind him, Rudolph's nose glowed steady and true.

A light that had guided through fog and storm and doubt for seventy-three years.

A light that would keep glowing whether anyone believed in it or not.

Because that's what lights do.

They shine.

Regardless.

CHAPTER 9
"JUST SHOW UP"

~

December 24th, 7:00 PM - Pre-Flight

The air tasted like Christmas Eve.

That particular cold that sits in your lungs and makes every breath visible. Sharp. Clean. Smelling of snow and pine and that indefinable something that only exists on this one night.

Santa stood beside the sleigh, checking the harness connections for the third time. His hands moved on autopilot—seventy-three years of this same routine, muscle memory so deep it didn't require thought.

But his mind wasn't quiet.

The phone sat in the glove box. Powered off. But he could feel it there. Like a presence. Like a weight.

Seven hours ago, the algorithm had published.

He knew because Mrs. Claus had told him. Gently. Over the comm.

"It's out, dear. The article went live at 5:47 PM. I'm... I'm not going to tell you what it says."

"That bad?"

"That predictable. 'Santa's Surveillance State.' 'Big Brother in a Red Suit.' The usual." She'd paused. "Kris, you made the right choice. Turning off the phone. Not looking. That was right."

"Then why does it feel like running away?"

"Because you're brave enough to know the difference between surrender and wisdom."

That was two hours ago.

Now the sleigh was loaded. Rudolph was harnessed. The other reindeer—Dasher, Dancer, Prancer, Vixen, Comet, Cupid, Donner, Blitzen—all stood ready, breath steaming in the cold.

The northern lights had started early tonight. Green ribbons dancing across the sky, like the earth itself was celebrating.

Everything was ready.

Except him.

Santa climbed into the sleigh. Sat in the driver's seat. Put his hands on the reins.

And couldn't make himself say the word.

The word that would launch them. The word that would start the most important night of the year.

Because once he launched, there was no stopping. No checking. No knowing what the world was saying about him while he worked.

Four billion homes. Sixteen hours of flying. Complete radio silence except for Mrs. Claus on the emergency channel.

Flying blind.

Not just literally—though that was part of it, trusting Rudolph's nose through fog and storm.

But metaphorically blind. Not knowing if the algorithm article was destroying him. Not knowing if the chimney video had convinced anyone. Not knowing if—

"Santa?" Jinglebert's voice crackled through the comm. "We're at T-minus 5 minutes. Everything okay?"

Santa opened his mouth to answer.

The glove box caught his eye.

"Yeah," he said. "Everything's fine."

But it wasn't.

7:02 PM - THE TEMPTATION

"Sir?" Jinglebert again. "I have the final engagement metrics if you want them. Before you go dark."

Santa's hand moved toward the glove box.

Stopped.

"What are they?"

"The chimney video is at 8.2 million views. Sentiment analysis shows..." Jinglebert's voice got quieter. "73% still don't believe it's real. But engagement is high. Comments are active. The algorithm article has been shared 400,000 times. And, um. There's been some interesting comments in the last hour."

Santa's fingers touched the glove box latch.

"Interesting how?"

"I think you should see them yourself, sir."

"Jinglebert. I'm about to launch. I'm about to go dark for sixteen hours. If there's something I need to know—"

"It's not urgent, sir. It's just... one comment in particular. On your last post. The 'believe or don't' post."

Santa's thumb pressed against the latch.

He could open it. Power on the phone. Read one comment. Just one.

What would it hurt?

"What does it say?" he asked.

Silence on the comm.

Then Mrs. Claus's voice, gentle: "Kris. Don't."

"Martha—"

"Whatever's in those comments, whatever's happening online right now—it doesn't change the work. You know that. We just talked about this."

"I know, but—"

"You made a choice two hours ago. A hard choice. Don't unmake it now."

Rudolph turned his head. Looked back at Santa. His nose glowed steady, patient.

You going to do this or not? his expression said. Because I'm ready. Question is: are you?

Santa's hand fell away from the glove box.

"You're right," he said. "You're right. I'm sorry. I just—"

"I know," Mrs. Claus said. "I know it's hard. But you're doing the right thing."

"Jinglebert," Santa said. "I don't need the metrics. Whatever that comment says, I'll read it tomorrow. Tonight, I work."

"Copy that, sir. But... if it helps? I think you'd like this one. It's from a kid. Seven years old. And it's... it's really something."

Santa closed his eyes.

A kid.

Seven years old.

The age when belief still comes easy. When magic doesn't need proof. When Santa is simply real because of course he is.

"Read it to me," he said quietly.

7:05 PM - THE WISDOM OF A CHILD

Jinglebert's voice came through, reading slowly:

"Posted by @LittleTimmy_Age7, at 6:47 PM: 'why would the real santa need to prove hes real? if youre real you just ARE real. like my mom is real. she doesnt have to prove shes my mom. she just IS. santa if youre reading this you dont have to proof anything. i beleeve in you because you show up. thats all. just show up. love timmy.'"

The comm went silent.

Santa sat very still.

Read it again in his head. Slower this time.

Why would the real Santa need to prove he's real?

If you're real you just ARE real.

You don't have to proof anything.

Just show up.

Seven years old.

This child—this child—had cut through two thousand years of anxiety with four simple sentences.

Why would the real Santa need to prove he's real?

And something happened in Santa's body.

Started in his chest—that tight knot of anxiety that had been living there all day, wound tighter and tighter with every comment, every view, every moment of desperate proving—it loosened.

Not all at once.

Slowly.

Like a fist unclenching. Like a rope unwinding. Like ice melting in spring sun.

The tightness spread outward as it released. Down his arms. Into his hands. The trembling that had plagued him all day—gone. Just... gone.

His shoulders dropped. He hadn't realized how high he'd been holding them. How much tension he'd been carrying. But now they fell, and it was like setting down a pack he'd been hauling up a mountain.

His breathing deepened. Slowed. Became real breath instead of the shallow, anxious gasps he'd been surviving on.

The weight in his chest—the one he'd been carrying since 6 AM this morning, since that first post went live, since he'd stepped onto this impossible path of proving himself—lifted.

Actually lifted.

Like gravity had decided to be kind for once.

"Sir?" Jinglebert's voice was uncertain. "You still there?"

Santa's hands were shaking.

Not from fear.

From something else.

Relief?

Recognition?

Liberation?

"Say it again," Santa whispered. "The first part."

"'Why would the real Santa need to prove he's real?'"

Santa's breath came out in a visible cloud. He watched it dissipate into the night air.

Why would the real Santa need to prove he's real?

Because he'd forgotten.

Somewhere in the panic and the algorithm and the comments and the metrics and the desperate need for validation—he'd forgotten the simplest truth.

Real things don't need proof.

They just ARE.

His mother didn't need to prove she was his mother. She just was.

The stars didn't need to prove they were stars. They just were.

Love didn't need to prove it was love. It just was.

And Santa—real, exhausted, seventeen-hundred-year-old Santa, sitting in a sleigh on Christmas Eve with a bag full of presents and a heart full of hope—didn't need to prove he was real.

He just was.

"Oh," Santa said softly.

The word felt small in his mouth. Insufficient. Like trying to describe sunrise with a single syllable.

But it was the sound of understanding arriving. Of truth landing. Of the final puzzle piece clicking into place.

And then it hit him. Really hit him.

Not in his mind—he'd understood it intellectually the moment Jinglebert read the comment.

But now it hit his BODY. His BONES. His SOUL.

He didn't need to prove anything.

He WAS real.

He had ALWAYS been real.

Nothing that had happened today—no comment, no view, no explanation, no mockery—had changed that fundamental truth.

He was real.

And he'd spent an entire day trying to convince strangers of something that was simply, undeniably, irrevocably TRUE.

"Oh," he said again.

And then, louder: "Oh."

And then he started laughing.

Not the broken, bitter laugh from earlier. Not the desperate edge-of-panic sound.

Real laughter. Deep. From the belly. The kind that makes your shoulders shake and your eyes water and your whole body participate in the joy.

"Sir?" Jinglebert sounded alarmed. "Are you okay?"

"I'm an idiot," Santa gasped between laughs. "I'm a complete and total idiot."

"Um—"

"I spent all day trying to prove I'm real to people who are determined not to believe. I let a seven-year-old understand something I forgot. I —" Another wave of laughter. "I let strangers make me doubt MYSELF. Me! Santa Claus! Who's been doing this job since the year 336!"

Mrs. Claus's voice came through, warm with relief and amusement: "There he is."

"Martha, did you hear what this kid said?"

"I heard."

"A SEVEN-YEAR-OLD figured out what I couldn't. Just show up. That's all. That's EVERYTHING."

"Yes."

"I don't need to prove anything."

"No."

"I just need to BE. To do the work. To show up."

"Yes, Kris. Yes."

Santa wiped his eyes. His hands had stopped shaking. His chest felt lighter. Lighter than it had felt in years, maybe. Like he'd been carrying this weight for longer than just today. Like maybe he'd been trying to prove himself for decades and had only just now realized he could stop.

The weight he'd been carrying—the desperate need to be believed, to be validated, to be seen and recognized and real in the eyes of strangers—it was falling away. Like snow sliding off a roof. Like chains breaking. Like prison doors opening.

He looked at the glove box.

At the phone inside.

And for the first time all day, he didn't feel its pull.

"Jinglebert," he said.

"Yes, sir?"

"Can you access my account from your end?"

"Of course, sir."

"Good. I want you to post something for me. Right now."

"What should it say?"

Santa thought for a moment.

Then smiled.

~

7:10 PM - THE FINAL POST

The post went live at 7:11 PM:

To @LittleTimmy_Age7: You're right. I don't need to prove I'm real. I just need to show up. Thank you for reminding me. I'll see you tonight.

To everyone else: Believe or don't. Either way, I have work to do. Merry Christmas. 

That was it.

No livestream announcement. No "follow my journey." No "check back tomorrow for proof."

Just: I have work to do.

"Post it," Santa said.

"Done, sir. It's live."

"Good. Now shut down the account."

Jinglebert's voice went up an octave: "Shut it DOWN?"

"Not permanently. Just... put it in vacation mode. Auto-reply to messages saying I'll be back after Christmas. Turn off all notifications. Make it go dark."

"But sir, what if people want to—"

"They can want. I have deliveries to make."

A pause.

Then, quietly: "Yes, sir. Shutting it down now."

Santa could picture it: the Instagram account going silent. The blue checkmark still there, but the account dormant. Like closing a door.

Not locked.

Just... closed.

Private.

His.

"It's done," Jinglebert said. "Account is dark. You won't get any notifications. Nobody can reach you. You're officially off the grid."

"Perfect."

"Sir? Can I say something?"

"Of course."

"I think..." Jinglebert's voice cracked slightly. "I think I learned something today. About what matters. And I'm sorry I pushed you so hard toward the metrics. Toward proving yourself. That was wrong."

Santa's expression softened. "You were trying to help."

"I was trying to win. That's different."

"Yes. It is. But you learned. That's what matters."

"Will you... will you still want my help? After tonight? After I pushed you into all this?"

"Jinglebert." Santa's voice was firm but kind. "You're 89 years old. You made a mistake. You learned from it. We all did. And yes, I'll still want your help. But next year? We do things differently."

"How?"

"We remember what that child said. We just show up. The rest takes care of itself."

Silence. Then: "Yes, sir. I'll remember."

"Good. Now I need to fly."

"Godspeed, Santa. And sir?"

"Yeah?"

"Thank you. For teaching me."

The comm clicked off.

~

7:15 PM - THE LAUNCH

Santa stood up in the sleigh. The runners creaked beneath his weight —old wood, older magic, oldest trust.

Rudolph looked back at him. The other reindeer shifted, ready.

Mrs. Claus's face appeared on the dash screen one final time.

"You good?" she asked.

He looked at her. At the woman who'd seen him at his worst today.

Who'd held him together when he was falling apart. Who'd believed in him when he'd stopped believing in himself.

"I'm good," he said.

"You sure?"

"Yeah. I'm sure. I know what I'm doing now."

"Which is?"

"My job. The real job. Not the performance. Not the proof. Just... the work."

She smiled. That smile that still made his heart skip after four hundred years.

"Go do your work, Kris. The real work."

He nodded.

She blew him a kiss.

The screen went dark.

Santa looked down at the glove box one more time.

The phone sat inside. Powered off. Silent. Waiting.

He could take it with him. Just in case. Just for emergencies. Just to have it there, that connection to the outside world, that window to millions of strangers who might or might not believe.

His hand rested on the glove box.

But he didn't open it.

Because here's what he understood now, what Timmy's simple wisdom had unlocked:

The phone wasn't just a device. It was a temptation. It was the embodied form of his need to be validated, to be seen, to be proven real by strangers who would never know him.

And every time he checked it—every scroll, every refresh, every compulsive glance at metrics—he was choosing their opinion over his own knowing.

He was choosing external validation over internal truth.

He was choosing proof over presence.

And he was done choosing that.

The phone would still be there tomorrow.

The comments would still be there tomorrow.

The 8.2 million views would still be there tomorrow.

But tonight?

Tonight there was only the work.

Tonight there was only showing up.

Tonight there was only being real, regardless of who believed it.

Santa's hand lifted from the glove box.

Left it closed.

Left the phone inside, dormant and distant.

It felt like the most important choice he'd made all day.

Maybe all year.

Maybe ever.

He looked at Rudolph. Met his eyes in the darkness.

"Ready?" Santa asked.

Rudolph's nose flared brilliant red.

Not for cameras.

Not for TikTok.

Not for proof.

For the work.

For the children.

For the magic that existed whether anyone believed in it or not.

"Let's go," Santa said.

And snapped the reins.

~

7:16 PM - INTO THE DARK

The sleigh lifted.

No countdown.

No livestream.

No cameras recording for posterity.

Just the creak of runners leaving snow—that specific sound, like a sigh, like release, like the earth letting go of what it held.

The whoosh of reindeer hooves finding air—not beating, not flapping, just... finding purchase on something invisible, something impossible, something that only existed because magic did.

The rush of wind as they climbed—cold and sharp and alive, slapping Santa's face, filling his lungs, making his eyes water. Real wind. Solid and undeniable and carrying them up.

Santa felt it in his body: the moment of liftoff. That split-second between ground and sky. Between earth and flight. Between the weight of the world and the lightness of magic.

His stomach dropped—that carnival ride feeling, that trust-fall sensation.

His hands gripped the reins tighter—the leather warm from his palms despite the cold, familiar, solid.

His heart lifted—literally, physically lifted in his chest, rising with the sleigh, becoming weightless and heavy at once.

They rose.

The workshop fell away below. The elves—visible in the windows—waving. Torbin with his welding torch raised in salute. Buttons with a tray of fresh cookies held high. Their faces shrinking, becoming dots, becoming memory.

Higher.

The North Pole itself shrinking. The ice fields spreading out like a white ocean. The aurora borealis now around them instead of above them, green ribbons of light streaming past like they were flying through liquid emerald. The colors so bright they sang. So alive they breathed.

Higher.

Until there was only sky.

Stars so bright they hurt. Sharp pinpricks of ancient light, each one a sun, each one a world, each one saying: You are small. You are brief. You matter anyway.

Cold air so clean it burned. Searing his throat, shocking his lungs, making every breath a small miracle of survival and presence.

The curve of the earth visible below. That impossible arc. That proof of geometry and grace. The planet turning beneath them, oblivious and beautiful.

And silence.

Perfect, complete, sacred silence.

Not the absence of sound—there was sound. The wind howling. The runners creaking. The reindeer's hooves finding rhythm. His own breathing loud in his ears.

But silence underneath it all. The silence of being alone with the work. Of being present without audience. Of existing without proving existence.

No phone buzzing.

No comments loading.

No metrics updating.

No strangers judging.

Just Santa, his reindeer, the night sky, and four billion homes waiting below.

The work.

Pure.

Witnessed by no one.

Magnificent regardless.

And in that silence, Santa found something he'd been missing all day.

Peace.

Not the peace of resolution—nothing was resolved. The comments were still there. The doubters still doubted. The algorithm article still called him surveillance.

But the peace of purpose. The peace of knowing. The peace of being real whether anyone acknowledged it or not.

The peace of simply BEING.

He existed.

He was flying.

He was real.

And that was enough.

More than enough.

Everything.

Santa breathed in the cold air. Let it fill him completely. Let it wake every nerve, every cell, every part of him that had been numb with anxiety and desperation.

He was ALIVE.

He was REAL.

He was HERE.

And whether anyone believed that or not?

It didn't change a single thing.

"First stop," he called to Rudolph. "Tokyo. Three hundred thousand homes. You know the route."

Rudolph's nose brightened in acknowledgment.

They banked east.

The stars wheeled overhead.

And below them, the world slept, unaware that magic was about to visit.

7:45 PM - NORTH POLE GROUND

Mrs. Claus stood in the snow outside the workshop, watching until the sleigh was just a red dot in the sky.

Then not even that.

Just stars.

Just night.

Just the northern lights dancing their eternal dance.

Jinglebert came to stand beside her, tablet in hand.

"He's gone," Jinglebert said unnecessarily.

"He is."

"The account's getting a lot of engagement on that last post."

"Of course it is."

"The kid—Timmy—he replied. Said 'your welcome mr santa i knew youd understand.'"

Mrs. Claus smiled. "Wise child."

"Do you think..." Jinglebert hesitated. "Do you think what we did today was worth it? All the stress, the panic, the comments? Did we learn anything?"

Mrs. Claus was quiet for a moment. Then: "We learned that proof is the opposite of faith. That validation from strangers is a trap. That the work is the point, not the applause. That love doesn't need an audience." She looked at him. "So yes. We learned. And it hurt. But that doesn't mean it wasn't worth it."

"Will he do social media again? Next year?"

"Maybe. Maybe not. But if he does, it'll be different. He'll remember what that child said. He'll remember what he forgot today."

"What did he forget?"

"That real things don't need proof. They just are."

Jinglebert looked at his tablet. At the engagement metrics still climbing. At the comments still loading.

Then he powered it off.

"I think I'll remember that too," he said quietly.

Mrs. Claus put her arm around his shoulders. "Good. Now come inside. We have cookies to eat and cocoa to drink and sixteen hours to wait. And Jinglebert?"

"Yes, ma'am?"

"No checking the metrics. Not tonight. Tonight we trust the work. We trust him. We trust that showing up is enough."

"Even if nobody sees?"

"Especially if nobody sees. That's when it matters most."

They walked back toward the workshop together.

Behind them, the northern lights danced on.

The most beautiful show on earth.

Seen by almost no one.

Magnificent regardless.

～

7:50 PM - THE AIR SOMEWHERE OVER THE PACIFIC

Santa flew in silence.

The reindeer's hooves made no sound. Magic muffled everything—the rush of wind, the creak of sleigh, even his own breathing seemed distant.

Below: ocean. Vast. Dark. Dotted with the lights of ships.

Above: stars. Infinite. Indifferent. Beautiful.

And in his chest: peace.

Real peace.

Not the absence of fear.

Not the absence of doubt.

But the presence of purpose.

He thought about Timmy's comment. Just show up. That's all.

And he thought about all the years before social media. Before smartphones. Before livestreams and engagement metrics and viral videos.

Back when he just... showed up.

Went down chimneys. Left presents. Ate cookies. Drank milk.

No proof.

No cameras.

No validation.

Just the work.

And it had been enough.

It had always been enough.

Somewhere below, a child was sleeping. Maybe dreaming. Maybe scared. Maybe lonely. Maybe hoping that tomorrow morning, there would be a sign that someone out there cared.

And there would be.

Not because Santa needed to prove himself.

But because that's what love does.

It shows up.

Regardless of applause.

Regardless of belief.

Regardless of proof.

It just shows up.

Santa smiled into the darkness.

"Thank you, Timmy," he whispered.

The wind carried his words away.

The stars kept shining.

The sleigh kept flying.

And the work—the real, sacred, beautiful work—continued.

Whether anyone saw it or not.

Because that's what real things do.

They exist.

They persist.

They ARE.

Proof not required.

Faith not demanded.

Just...

Present.

Always present.

Always real.

Always showing up.

CHAPTER 10
"THE DELIVERY"

~

December 24th, 8:00 PM - Midnight

The Air

The cold was absolute.

Not the comfortable winter-sweater cold of a December afternoon. Not even the sharp sting of January mornings when you stepped outside and your breath caught. This was different. This was the cold of altitude, of atmosphere, of flying through air so thin and frozen it felt like breathing knives.

Santa's lungs burned with each inhale. The air cut going down. Sharp. Immediate. His exhales came out in clouds so thick they obscured his vision for seconds at a time, forcing him to navigate blind through the space between breaths.

He'd learned, over seventeen centuries, to time his breathing with the rhythm of flight. Inhale during the glide when the air was steadier.

Exhale on the descent when the pressure changed. Hold during the turns when his body needed all its strength just to stay in the sleigh.

It was muscle memory now. Like walking. Like blinking.

Like living.

It was 8:47 PM when they reached the first house.

Tokyo. Shibuya district. Fourteenth floor of a high-rise apartment building. No chimney—just a balcony door and the magic that made locked things unlocked, solid things permeable, impossible things routine.

Santa's hands shook as he guided the sleigh to hover beside the balcony.

Not from cold—though his fingers were already numb inside the red gloves, the leather stiff and unyielding.

From something else.

The work.

The weight of it.

Four billion homes stretched before him like an infinite to-do list. Each one a universe of need. Each one a story unfolding in real time. Each one mattering completely.

How do you carry four billion stories?

How do you hold that much need without collapsing under it?

His knees protested as he stood. Seventeen hundred years of Christmas Eves had left their mark—the cartilage worn thin, the joints stiff in the cold, little bone spurs that caught and scraped with every movement. His doctor (yes, Santa had a doctor) had suggested knee replacement surgery three centuries ago.

Santa had laughed.

"Who has time for recovery?"

The knees held. They always held. They had to.

He stepped onto the balcony. Felt the magic do its thing—the door opening without opening, reality bending just enough to let him through, his body slipping through glass like a ghost. The physics of the world treating him as exception. As special case. As the one thing that didn't have to follow the rules.

Inside: a small apartment. Neat. Sparse in the way that spoke of careful budgeting and thoughtful choices. Not poverty exactly, but the constant awareness of every yen spent.

A single mother and her daughter, both sleeping in the same bed. Not because there wasn't a second bedroom—there was, barely bigger than a closet. But because sleeping together was warmer. Cheaper. Because the heater cost money and body heat was free.

The Christmas tree stood in the corner. Artificial. Three feet tall. The kind you could buy at a convenience store. But decorated with love— paper ornaments the daughter had made. Construction paper snowflakes, each one unique. Hand-drawn candy canes in marker. One angel at the top made from a toilet paper roll and aluminum foil, her wings slightly crooked but trying so hard.

Beautiful.

So beautiful it hurt.

Santa stood there for a moment. Just looking. Just seeing.

This was what people missed when they asked "is Santa real?" They missed this. The seeing. The knowing. The caring about a paper angel made from a toilet paper roll.

His knees cracked as he knelt beside the tree—audible in the quiet apartment, loud enough that he winced and froze, waiting to see if he'd woken them.

They didn't stir.

He pulled the presents from his bag. Real toys from the workshop. Handmade. Wooden doll with joints that moved. Stuffed animals with button eyes. Wrapped in paper that shimmered with northern lights—green and purple and dancing even in the dim apartment light.

He arranged them carefully under the tree. Made sure they'd be visible first thing when the girl woke up.

Then he saw it.

The daughter's Christmas list. Taped to the refrigerator with Hello Kitty magnets.

Written in careful English (she was learning at school, practicing her letters):

Doll for me

Warm coat for Mama

Happiness

Santa stopped breathing.

Read it again.

That third item.

Happiness.

Not a toy. Not a thing you could wrap. Just... happiness.

What do you get someone who asks for happiness?

Santa's throat tightened. His chest hurt. Not the physical hurt from the cold. Something deeper. The ache of seeing someone who understood that things didn't matter if the people you loved were struggling.

This girl was seven years old and asking for happiness for her family.

Seven years old and already understanding what most adults forgot.

He reached into his bag. Deeper this time. Past the toys and games. Into the section that held the impossible gifts. The ones that couldn't be bought or built. The ones that required phone calls and favors and promises made centuries ago.

He pulled out an envelope.

Inside: a job offer letter. Printed on official hospital letterhead. Dated January 2nd. The hospital where the mother worked as a night janitor, mopping floors while her daughter slept, offering her a daytime nursing assistant position.

More money. Better hours. Home for dinner. Home to help with homework. Home to be MOM instead of just PROVIDER.

He'd pulled strings for this one. Called in a favor from the Japanese Minister of Health (who owed Santa since 1987 when Santa had helped his daughter during a particularly difficult time). Made sure the offer would arrive at exactly the right moment. Made sure it was real, official, legitimate.

Would it bring happiness?

Maybe.

Maybe not.

Happiness was complicated. Couldn't be guaranteed. Couldn't be bought or delivered or wrapped in shimmering paper.

But it was what he could do.

It was something.

Santa placed the envelope on the counter where she'd see it first thing. Weighted it down with a small wooden reindeer from his pocket—Torbin's work, polished maple, perfect in its simplicity.

Then he stood. His knees screaming. His back protesting.

Left the way he came. Through glass. Through magic. Through the space between what is and what could be.

Back in the sleigh, he marked the house complete in his mental log.

One down.

3,999,999,999 to go.

The stars overhead were so bright they cast shadows. Real shadows on the sleigh floor. Like the sun but cold. Distant. Indifferent to the work happening below.

His fingers trembled as he picked up the reins again. Just slightly. Just enough to notice.

9:15 PM - SOMEWHERE OVER THE PACIFIC

The rhythm settled in.

Descend. Enter. Deliver. Ascend.

Descend. Enter. Deliver. Ascend.

House after house after house.

Seoul. Beijing. Sydney. Mumbai.

The world spun beneath them, a billion lights against the dark. Each light a home. Each home a story. Each story mattering.

By house one hundred, Santa's shoulders had begun to ache. A dull throb that pulsed with each movement of the bag. The straps cutting into the muscle. The weight pressing down in a way that made his spine compress.

By house two hundred, his lower back had joined the chorus. Sharp jabs when he bent. Spasms when he twisted. The kind of pain that made you gasp and freeze and have to breathe through it before you could move again.

By house three hundred, he was moving slower. Each chimney descent took longer. Each climb back up required more effort. His breathing came heavier, ragged, like he'd been running instead of flying.

By house five hundred, he was feeling every one of his seventeen hundred years.

The bag never got lighter—magic kept it full, always full, infinite toys for infinite children—but the weight of it pressed against his spine, his hips, his knees. Each house added not physical weight but something else.

Something heavier.

The weight of seeing. Of knowing. Of caring about every single one.

The Japanese mother waking up to a job offer.

The Korean boy finding the art supplies he'd been afraid to ask for.

The Chinese girl discovering the books she needed for school.

The Australian family opening presents they thought they couldn't afford.

All of it mattering.

All of it SEEN.

All of it weighing on Santa's shoulders like stones.

But he kept moving.

Because this was the work.

This was what showing up looked like.

Not cameras. Not comments. Not proof.

Just this.

The silent, invisible, witnessed-by-no-one act of delivering hope to sleeping children.

And then, at 9:43 PM, somewhere over Australia, he reached the first house that mattered differently.

Marcus's house.

The @SkibidiRizzler himself.

Fourteen years old. Suburban America. Two-story house with a three-car garage and a basketball hoop in the driveway and the kind of perfect exterior that hid everything falling apart inside.

Parents divorcing but not admitting it yet. The kind of slow-motion family death where everyone pretends everything's fine while the foundation crumbles beneath them.

Santa stood on the roof, looking at the chimney.

His hands were shaking worse now. Not just trembling. Shaking. His legs felt unsteady beneath him. Six hundred seventeen houses had taken their toll.

This was the boy who'd called him fake. Called the chimney video CGI. Called his reindeer an "Amazon LED special."

The boy who'd hurt Rudolph with his casual cruelty. Who'd made Santa doubt himself. Who'd represented everything wrong with the internet—the skepticism, the mockery, the refusal to believe in anything.

The boy who needed help anyway.

Because need didn't care about belief.

Because Santa showed up for everyone.

Even the ones who hurt him.

Santa took a breath. The cold air burned his lungs.

Then he went down the chimney.

9:45 PM - MARCUS'S HOUSE

The living room was dark except for the tree lights. Blue and white LEDs. Modern. Cold. The kind that looked good in photos but gave no warmth.

But the room itself... the room told the real story.

Two recliners facing the TV. Positioned at angles that meant the people sitting in them didn't have to look at each other. Didn't have to acknowledge each other. Could exist in the same space while being completely separate.

A coffee table covered in separate piles. His magazines about golf and cars. Her books about self-help and finding yourself. Neutral territory in between, carefully maintained, neither one crossing the invisible line.

Photos on the wall showed the family's history in reverse. Like watching a relationship die in snapshots:

Young parents, clearly in love, Marcus as a baby. Both of them looking at the camera like they'd won the lottery.

Marcus at five, both parents smiling. Real smiles. The kind that use your whole face.

Marcus at eight, the smiles getting tighter. More performative. The kind you do because the photographer says "smile" not because you feel it.

Marcus at ten, taken at a studio because they'd stopped taking candid photos. Because candid meant spontaneous meant together meant something they weren't anymore.

Marcus at twelve, and you could see it—the distance between the parents, the careful space, the way they weren't touching even in a family portrait. Even when the photographer probably said "get closer."

No photo from this year.

No photo because they couldn't pretend anymore. Couldn't smile for the camera. Couldn't stand that close without the truth showing.

Santa's chest tightened. Not the physical tightness from earlier. This was different. This was the ache of recognizing pain. Of seeing a family breaking and knowing you could only do so much.

Knowing that some things couldn't be fixed with presents.

He moved through the house quietly. Up the stairs. Past the parents' bedroom—separate sides of the bed, bodies turned away from each other even in sleep, the space between them like a chasm.

Past the guest room where the father had been sleeping for the last month, though they were calling it "back problems."

To Marcus's room.

The door was cracked open. Inside: typical teenage chaos. Clothes on the floor in layers, like sediment. Gaming setup on the desk, three monitors, RGB lights, the glow never quite off. Posters of streamers and memes and inside jokes Santa didn't understand.

And on the wall beside his bed, carefully placed where he'd see it every morning and every night: a single photo.

Small. Printed on regular paper. Taped up with scotch tape that was starting to yellow.

His parents. From maybe eight years ago. At the beach. His dad's arm around his mom's waist. Both of them laughing—really laughing—at something little Marcus (visible in the frame's edge) had just said.

They'd been happy once.

Marcus knew they'd been happy once.

That's what made it hurt so much.

Not the anger. Anger you could fight against. Anger was energy. Anger meant you still cared enough to feel something.

But this quiet dissolution? This slow fade from love to coexistence to separate recliners?

This was worse.

This was watching happiness die in real time and being unable to stop it.

Santa looked at the boy sleeping in the bed. Fourteen years old. Pretending to be tough on the internet. Making jokes about deepfakes and CGI and Amazon LEDs because jokes were safer than hope.

But hoping anyway.

Hoping someone would see that he needed his family back.

Hoping magic was real.

Hoping Santa could fix what his parents had broken.

This hurt differently than the first house. The Japanese mother and daughter—that was poverty, that was circumstance, that was something external that could be fixed with a job offer and a wooden reindeer and a little bit of string-pulling.

But this?

This was people choosing to hurt each other. Choosing to give up. Choosing silence over fighting for what they'd once had.

This was harder to fix.

Maybe impossible to fix.

But Santa had to try anyway.

He reached into his bag.

The gift he pulled out wasn't wrapped. It was just a photo. The same photo from Marcus's wall—but the original. The actual photograph from eight years ago, edges worn from being held, a slight curve from where it had lived in someone's wallet.

The father's wallet. Santa had... borrowed... it from the man's desk. Found this photo tucked behind his credit cards. Creased from being taken out and looked at and put back. Evidence that the man still remembered. Still cared. Still loved the woman sleeping thirty feet away but might as well be on another planet.

But that wasn't all.

There was a note attached. Written in the father's handwriting (Santa had borrowed a sample from a grocery list):

Marcus - I found this in a box in the garage last night. Couldn't sleep, went looking for the Christmas lights, found this instead. Made me remember. Your mom and I are going to talk. Really talk. I don't know if we can fix this. But we're going to try. Because you deserve better than two people pretending. You deserve better than what we've been giving you. I'm sorry we forgot how to be happy. We're going to try to remember. Love, Dad.

Santa placed the photo and note on Marcus's nightstand. Right where he'd see it first thing in the morning. Right where it would be impossible to miss.

Would it work?

Would the parents actually talk?

Would one photo and one note undo months of silence and resentment and slow emotional death?

He didn't know.

But he'd seen something two weeks ago. At 3 AM when he'd been doing his pre-Christmas surveillance. The mother, alone in the kitchen, unable to sleep. Scrolling through photos on her phone. Old photos. Happy photos. Stopping on that beach photo. Zooming in on her husband's face. Whispering "I miss you" to a picture of a man sleeping thirty feet away.

They weren't done. Not quite. Not yet.

They just needed... a push. A reminder. A reason to try.

Maybe this would be it.

Maybe not.

But it was what he could do.

It was something.

Santa stood there for a moment longer, looking at Marcus. At this kid who'd called him fake, who'd hurt Rudolph, who was just scared and angry and fourteen and caught in the middle of something he didn't create and couldn't fix.

"I see you," Santa whispered into the dark room. His voice rough. Raw. The words feeling heavy. Important. Like a vow. "I see you, Marcus. And you're going to be okay. One way or another. You're going to be okay."

He meant it.

Even if Marcus's parents didn't fix their marriage. Even if they divorced. Even if this family broke apart completely.

Marcus would be okay.

Because someone had seen him. Because his pain mattered. Because he wasn't alone.

That had to count for something.

Then Santa left. Back down the stairs. Past the parents sleeping separately. Past the separate recliners and the photos showing love dying.

Out through the front door.

Into the cold.

Into the work.

His chest still ached. But differently now. Like it had absorbed some of Marcus's pain and was carrying it for him. Just for tonight. Just until morning when the boy would wake up and maybe—just maybe—things would be different.

10:02 PM - THE SLEIGH

"How many?" Mrs. Claus's voice came through the comm. She checked in every hour. Just to hear his voice. To make sure he was still himself. Still breathing. Still going.

"Seven hundred forty-three," Santa said. His voice was hoarse. Ragged. The cold did that. And the talking. And seventeen centuries of Christmas Eves.

"You sound tired."

"I am tired."

"Do you need to rest?"

"No. I need to keep going."

A pause on the other end. He could hear her breathing. Could picture her in the control room, surrounded by monitors, watching his progress across the globe.

"I love you," she said softly.

"I love you too."

The comm went quiet again.

Rudolph looked back at him from his position at the front of the sleigh. Those ancient eyes. That knowing look.

You good?

Santa nodded, but his hands told a different story—cramping now, the fingers stiff inside the gloves, joints that didn't want to bend properly. "Next stop. Seattle."

Rudolph's nose flared bright.

They banked west.

10:15 PM - DANNY'S APARTMENT

Fourteenth floor. Studio apartment. One person. One desk. One laptop. One bed.

The loneliness was visible in the negative space. In what wasn't there.

No photos on the walls. No decorations. No Christmas tree. No signs that another human ever visited this space. No second chair at the table. No extra toothbrush in the bathroom. No shoes by the door that weren't his.

Just work. Just code. Just... existing.

Danny—@TechBro9000—lay in bed, facing the wall. Not sleeping. Just lying there. Staring at nothing in the dark.

On the desk: an open laptop, three monitors, code on every screen. Even at 10 PM on Christmas Eve, code on every screen. Always working. Work as escape. Work as meaning. Work as substitute for human connection.

And on the desk, visible in the glow of the monitors, the browser history Santa could see reflected in the dark screen: a drafted email. To Emily. The sister he hadn't spoken to in five years.

The email Danny had written and deleted seventeen times in the last month alone:

Em,

I miss you. I'm sorry. Can we—

Deleted.

Emily,

I know it's been a long time, but—

Deleted.

Hey sis,

I was thinking about—

Deleted.

How many times had Danny written that email?

How many times had he typed "I miss you" and then convinced himself that Emily had moved on, that she didn't want to hear from him, that reaching out would just make things worse?

How many times had he chosen loneliness over the risk of rejection?

Santa stood in the doorway of this suffocating space, and the loneliness hit him like a physical thing. Like walking into a wall of cold air. Like stepping into a tomb where someone had been buried alive.

This was different from Marcus's house.

Marcus's pain was loud—a family falling apart, emotions everywhere, love turning to anger turning to silence. Marcus's pain was visible. Present. Shared.

But Danny's pain was quiet.

Suffocating.

The kind of loneliness that doesn't scream. It just... sits. Heavy. Crushing. Slowly squeezing the life out of you one isolated day at a time.

This was the loneliness of choice. Of being so scared of rejection that you choose solitude. Of deleting emails instead of sending them. Of convincing yourself that being alone is safer than risking connection.

Of waking up in an empty apartment and telling yourself this is what you want.

Santa's own chest felt tight just standing here. Like the apartment's isolation was contagious. Like he could feel the weight of five years of unsent emails, unmade phone calls, unspoken apologies pressing down on his lungs.

This boy was so lonely it was killing him.

Not quickly. Not dramatically. Not in any way that would show up on a medical exam.

Just slowly.

The way isolation kills—one deleted email at a time, one avoided call at a time, one day without real human contact at a time.

Until you forget what connection feels like.

Until you convince yourself you don't need it.

Until the loneliness becomes so normal you can't imagine anything else.

Santa reached into his bag.

The item he pulled out was delicate. An envelope. Old. The paper yellowed at the edges like something that had been kept in a drawer for years.

Inside: a letter. In Emily's handwriting. Dated three years ago.

Danny - I don't know if you'll ever read this. I don't know if you even want to hear from me. But I'm writing it anyway because if I don't, I'll regret it forever. I miss you. I miss my brother. I miss the person who taught me to code, who stayed up all night helping me with my calculus homework, who believed in me when no one else did. I don't know what happened to us. I don't know when we stopped talking. But I want to fix it. I want you back in my life. Call me. Please. Love, Em.

Santa had found this letter three years ago. In Emily's apartment. In her trash can, surrounded by crumpled drafts. She'd written it seventeen times before giving up, deciding that Danny wouldn't want to hear from her, that he'd moved on, that reaching out would just make things worse.

She'd been wrong.

He'd been writing the same email she'd been afraid to send.

They were both so scared of rejection they'd chosen five years of loneliness instead.

Five years of missing each other.

Five years of being alone when they didn't have to be.

Because neither one was brave enough to press send.

Santa placed the letter on Danny's pillow. Right beside his head. Where he couldn't miss it when he woke up.

Then he pulled out one more thing: a Post-It note. Written in Santa's own handwriting (neat, old-fashioned, the penmanship of someone who learned to write with a quill):

She wrote this but never sent it. She was scared you didn't want to hear from her. She was wrong. Call her. -S

Would Danny call?

Would Emily answer?

Would five years of silence break with one letter and one phone call?

Would they forgive each other for all the time they'd wasted being afraid?

Santa didn't know.

But he knew this: Danny needed to know he wasn't alone. Emily needed to know her brother still existed. They needed each other, even if they'd forgotten how to need.

Santa stood there for a moment, looking at this young man lying in the dark, surrounded by everything except what mattered.

The loneliness pressed against Santa's chest like a weight. Physical. Real. He wanted to fix this. Wanted to guarantee that Danny would call, that Emily would answer, that five years would dissolve in one conversation and they'd find their way back to each other.

But he couldn't guarantee anything.

He could only give them the chance. The nudge. The reminder that connection was possible.

Sometimes that was enough.

Sometimes it wasn't.

"You're not alone," Santa whispered into the suffocating quiet. His voice barely audible. A prayer more than a statement. "You were never alone. She's been missing you this whole time. Every single day. She's been missing you."

Then he left. Through the door. Into the hallway. Into the cold night air that felt almost welcoming after the crushing isolation of that apartment.

Back to the sleigh.

Back to the work.

His shoulders burned now. His back screamed. But he kept moving.

10:47 PM - SOMEWHERE OVER NORTH AMERICA

Santa's hands were shaking now.

Not from cold. He was past feeling the cold. His body had gone numb somewhere around house nine hundred. Now he was operating on something else. Something beyond physical.

Will, maybe.

Or stubbornness.

Or the understanding that three billion, nine hundred ninety-nine million houses were still waiting and stopping wasn't an option.

From something else.

From carrying all this. All these lives. All this need. All this hope.

Marcus and his breaking family. Danny and his crushing loneliness.

And still so many more to go.

By house one thousand, he'd developed a limp—his right knee refusing to bend properly, the joint locked in a way that made every step agony.

By house eleven hundred, his vision had started to blur at the edges—exhaustion and cold conspiring to narrow his field of vision to a tunnel, to a pinpoint, to just what was directly in front of him.

By house twelve hundred, he was moving on autopilot—body remembering the movements even when mind wanted to stop, muscle memory carrying him through because conscious thought had become too difficult.

His shoulders burned. His knees ached. His back screamed.

But he kept moving.

Because this was the work.

This was what love looked like.

Not the pretty version. Not the hallmark card version.

The real version.

The version that hurt.

11:03 PM - SARAH'S HOUSE

The house was chaos even at 11 PM.

Santa could see it from the outside, hovering in the sleigh above the suburban street: lights on in every room, toys scattered across the lawn (forgotten in the rush to get four kids bathed and into bed), a minivan in the driveway with a bumper sticker that read "Chaos Coordinator" and another that said "My other car is also full of goldfish crackers."

Inside would be worse.

He went down the chimney, his body protesting every movement.

The living room: exactly as expected. Toys everywhere. Not decoratively scattered—genuinely everywhere, like a tsunami of plastic had hit. Laundry piled on the couch, clean but unfolded. Dishes on the coffee table from a dinner that had probably been eaten in front of the TV because sitting at the table with four kids was a battlefield. The TV still on, forgotten, playing some kids' show to an empty room.

And Sarah—@MomOf4KidsNoSleep—asleep on the couch.

Still in her day clothes. Jeans and a t-shirt with stains she'd probably stopped noticing months ago. One hand still holding a toy she'd been trying to clean up. She'd just... stopped. Run out of energy mid-motion. Fallen asleep sitting up, slumped against the armrest.

The dark circles under her eyes were visible even in sleep.

The stress lines on her forehead hadn't relaxed.

The exhaustion visible in every line of her body—shoulders hunched, back curved, whole body seeming to fold in on itself like it was trying to take up less space, use less energy, exist more quietly.

Santa stood there, looking at her.

And felt it in his own chest. The echo of it. The bone-deep exhaustion of serving and serving and serving while everyone takes and takes and takes, never thinking to give back.

This was different from Danny's loneliness or Marcus's pain.

This wasn't isolation. This wasn't brokenness.

This was erasure.

This was someone who gave and gave and gave until there was nothing left. Until she'd become invisible even to herself. Until "Sarah" had disappeared entirely under the weight of "Mom."

When was the last time someone had called her by her name?

When was the last time someone had seen her as a person instead of a function?

Santa knew that exhaustion. Was feeling it right now, actually. House twelve hundred forty-seven and counting. The weight of all these people needing him.

But he could stop after tonight. Could rest tomorrow. Could spend December 26th sleeping and recovering and being taken care of by Martha.

Sarah couldn't stop. Ever.

There was no Christmas morning rest for mothers. No day off. No recovery period.

The kids would wake up at 6 AM. Would need breakfast. Would need supervision. Would need her to be present and patient and grateful and joyful because it was Christmas and you were supposed to be joyful on Christmas even if you were so tired you wanted to cry.

Just more. Always more.

This woman gave and gave and gave. To her children. To her husband. To everyone who needed her.

Who gave to her?

When was the last time someone had seen her? Really seen her? Not as Mom, not as Wife, not as the person who made everything work.

But as Sarah.

As a human being who was tired and scared and barely holding on.

Santa's eyes burned.

Not from the cold this time.

He moved through the house quietly. Stepping over toys. Around laundry piles. Through the lived-in chaos of a family that was functioning but just barely.

Up to the kids' rooms.

Four kids, ages 4, 7, 9, and 12.

Each one sleeping peacefully in beds Sarah had made. In rooms Sarah had cleaned. In a house Sarah held together through sheer force of will.

Completely unaware that their mother was downstairs running on fumes.

Completely unaware that she was drowning.

But Santa knew.

He'd been watching. Seen the Instagram posts that were all sunshine and "blessed" hashtags while the reality was dirty dishes and midnight crying sessions and googling "am I a bad mother" at 2 AM.

Seen her staring at herself in the mirror, mouthing "you can do this" like a prayer, like a mantra, like if she said it enough times it would become true.

She couldn't keep this up.

Something would break.

Maybe her. Probably her.

Santa went back downstairs. Stood beside the couch where she slept in her day clothes with a toy in her hand.

From his bag, he pulled a gift bag. Professional. Nice. Inside: a spa certificate. Four hours. Massage. Facial. Mani-pedi. The works. Purchased yesterday. Paid for by... well, Santa had a credit card. (Mrs. Claus handled the finances. He didn't ask questions.)

Four hours of someone else taking care of HER for once.

But that wasn't all.

There was a note.

And this one... this one had taken work.

Santa had reached out to Sarah's kids. All four of them. Through their tablets, through their school emails, through the magic that let him access what needed accessing when it mattered.

He'd sent them a message three days ago:

Your mom is tired. She won't say it because she thinks moms aren't supposed to be tired. But she is. She needs help. She needs rest. She needs to know you see her. Talk to your dad. Make a plan. Give her one day off. Just one day. She'll try to say no. Don't let her. She needs this. Love, Santa

All four kids had responded within hours:

ok

we can do that

is mom ok?

yes. we'll help

They'd already been planning it, Santa knew. Already pooling their allowance money. Already whispering about it when Sarah wasn't listening. Already noticing that Mom seemed different lately. Sadder. More tired. Less... there.

They just needed permission. Needed someone to tell them it was okay to notice that Mom was tired. That it wasn't selfish to think

Mom needed help. That taking care of her wasn't disrespectful or ungrateful.

It was love.

The note in the gift bag was from them:

Mom - We booked you a spa day. January 3rd. Dad's taking the day off. We're taking care of everything. You don't get to say no. We see you. We love you. Thank you for everything. - Your kids

All four signatures. Madison's careful cursive. James's awkward print. Emma's enthusiastic bubbles over the i's. Little Michael's name spelled wrong but so, so proud.

Santa placed the bag beside the couch. Right where she'd see it when she woke up to face another day of giving.

Then he did something he rarely did.

He knelt beside the couch.

His knees protested—cracking audibly in the quiet room, pain shooting up his legs. But he knelt anyway.

Put his hand on her shoulder. Very gently. Barely touching.

"You're doing great," he whispered. His voice was rough, raw from the cold and the hours and seventeen centuries of Christmas Eves. "You're doing so, so great. And you're not alone. They see you. I promise. They see you."

Sarah stirred slightly in her sleep.

Smiled.

Just a small movement at the corner of her mouth. But a smile.

And Santa felt something crack open in his chest. Not breaking. Opening. Like a door he'd kept locked swinging wide. Like something frozen beginning to thaw.

Because he understood this. The exhaustion. The invisible service. The giving until empty.

He was doing it right now. Had been doing it for seventeen hundred years.

And someone saw him. Mrs. Claus saw him. Timmy saw him. Even if the world didn't.

Just like Sarah's kids saw her. Even if she couldn't see it herself.

Santa stood—his knees screaming, his back seizing, his whole body rebelling against the movement. His vision swam. His hands were trembling violently now.

But he kept moving.

Because the work wasn't done.

It was never done.

11:34 PM - THE BREAKING POINT

Somewhere over Kansas, at 11:34 PM, Santa's body finally said no.

He'd just finished house number 1,247. A small farmhouse. Two kids. Easy delivery. Standard toys. Nothing complicated. In and out in four minutes.

But when he climbed back into the sleigh, his legs wouldn't hold him.

He collapsed onto the seat.

Not a controlled sit. Not tired-but-functional.

A collapse.

His knees buckling. His body giving out completely.

Breathing hard. Gasping. Each inhale like swallowing glass. Each exhale a shudder that wracked his entire frame.

His hands shook so violently he couldn't grip the reins. The trembling had spread to his whole body now—shoulders jerking, chest heaving, legs spasming.

The cold had worked its way into his bones. The exhaustion had become absolute. Seventeen hundred years of Christmas Eves, and this was the first time his body had actually given out.

Not just tired. Not just aching.

Failing.

Shutting down.

Saying no more. No further. This is too much.

The weight of all these lives, all this need, all this hope—

The Japanese mother and her daughter.

Marcus and his breaking family.

Danny and his crushing loneliness.

Sarah and her invisible exhaustion.

All of them and three billion, nine hundred ninety-eight million more still waiting—

It was too much.

It was too much and he couldn't—

His vision tunneled. Dark at the edges. Closing in like the world was narrowing to a pinpoint. Like consciousness was slipping away.

His chest seized—tight, impossibly tight, like his ribs had become a cage and his heart was trapped inside and couldn't beat properly and couldn't get enough oxygen and—

He couldn't breathe.

Couldn't think.

Couldn't—

"Martha," he gasped into the comm. His voice didn't sound like his voice. It sounded like someone dying. Someone drowning. Someone at the absolute end. "Martha, I can't—"

Her face appeared on the screen immediately.

Took one look at him—the pale face, the violent shaking, the eyes wide with something like panic, like terror, like the understanding that his body had finally reached its limit—

And her expression shifted from concern to alarm.

"Kris. Oh, Kris."

"I can't do this." His voice broke. Shattered. Became something raw and desperate and true. "There's so many of them. So many people hurting. Marcus and Danny and Sarah and Kevin and Timmy and—" He was crying now. Tears freezing on his cheeks before they could fall, crystallizing immediately in the altitude. "How do I help them all? How do I—"

"You can't," she said gently. Firmly. The only solid thing in a world that was spinning. "You can't help them all."

"Then what's the POINT?" he shouted.

The words ripped out of him. Seventeen hundred years of exhaustion in one scream. Seventeen hundred years of seeing need and trying to meet it and never being enough.

"What's the point of any of this if I can't—"

"You help the ones you can." Her voice was steady. Anchoring. The lifeline he needed. "That has to be enough."

"IS it enough?" Tears were freezing on his cheeks. His whole body was shaking. "Is it EVER enough?"

Silence.

Just the wind howling past the sleigh. Just his ragged breathing. Just the vast, indifferent sky.

Then: "I don't know, my love. I don't know if it's enough. But it's what we have. It's what you can do. And that has to matter."

Santa looked at his hands.

Shaking. Raw. The gloves torn at the seams. Blood on his knuckles from chimney bricks. Seventeen hundred years old and falling apart.

"I'm so tired, Martha." The words came out small. Broken. Honest. More honest than he'd been in centuries. "I'm so tired."

"I know."

"I don't know if I can keep going."

"You can."

"How do you know?"

"Because you always do. Every year. For seventeen hundred years. You always keep going."

He closed his eyes. Felt the cold burning his lungs. Felt the ache in every muscle, every bone, every cell. Felt the weight pressing down, down, down.

Three billion, nine hundred ninety-eight million, seven hundred fifty-three thousand homes still waiting.

Impossible.

It was impossible.

"I'm not doing this for the applause anymore," he said quietly. Eyes still closed. Voice barely audible over the wind. "I know that now. But Martha... it still hurts. Seeing all this pain. Knowing I can only fix such a small part of it. Knowing most of them will never even know I was there."

"Yes. It hurts. Love hurts. Caring hurts. Seeing people hurts." She paused. He heard her take a breath. "But that's not a reason to stop. That's the reason to continue."

Santa opened his eyes.

Looked at her face on the screen.

At the woman who'd been his anchor for four hundred years. Who'd seen him break before. Who'd always believed he'd put himself back together.

"I love you," he said.

"I love you too. Now breathe. Drink some water. Take five minutes. Then keep going."

"How many more?"

"Three billion, nine hundred ninety-eight million, seven hundred fifty-three thousand."

He laughed.

Actually laughed.

A broken, exhausted, slightly hysterical sound.

But a laugh.

"That's all?"

"That's all."

He drank water from the canteen beside his seat. The liquid shocking his system. Cold going down. Burning his frozen throat. But forcing awareness back into his body.

Took five deep breaths. Let the shaking slow. Let his vision clear. Let the panic recede just enough to function.

Then picked up the reins.

His hands still trembled. His body still screamed. But he could move. Could function. Could keep going.

"Okay," he said. "Okay. I can do this."

"I know you can."

"Kevin's next. Then Timmy. Then the rest."

"Then the rest," she agreed.

Santa looked at Rudolph. The reindeer had been watching. Waiting. Patient. That ancient red nose glowing steady.

Ready? Rudolph asked.

"Yeah," Santa said. "I'm ready."

They rose back into the sky.

Into the cold.

Into the work.

Continuing.

Always continuing.

Because that's what real things do.

They persist.

11:52 PM - KEVIN'S APARTMENT

The memorial corner stopped Santa in his tracks.

Photos of Kevin's parents. Everywhere. Young. Smiling. Alive.

Wedding photo. Honeymoon photo. First house photo. Kevin as a baby photo. First day of school photo. Birthday after birthday after birthday.

Candles burning. Careful arrangement. Fresh flowers—even in

December, Kevin kept fresh flowers there. Changed them every week. White roses. His mother's favorite.

Their wedding rings on a small velvet cushion. Polished. Cared for. Touched often, clearly. The gold worn smooth.

And Kevin himself, asleep in a chair beside his conspiracy boards.

Not asleep peacefully.

Asleep from exhaustion. From searching. From trying to make sense of a world that had taken his parents without reason, without warning, without mercy.

His laptop was still open on his lap. Reddit forum still visible. His latest post:

FIRE INVESTIGATION DISCREPANCIES: THREAD 847

Looking at chemical analysis from house fire 2018. Numbers don't add up. Someone explain...

173 comments. All of them variations of "I see it too" and "This doesn't make sense" and "WHAT ARE THEY HIDING."

Nothing.

They were hiding nothing.

Sometimes houses just catch fire. Sometimes the numbers are inconsistent because chaos doesn't follow patterns. Sometimes bad things happen and there's no conspiracy, no cover-up, no grand explanation that makes the pain make sense.

Sometimes love just ends in fire and smoke and there's no reason except bad luck and worse timing and a smoke detector that needed new batteries but got forgotten.

Santa looked at the boards.

Seven years of work. Red string connecting photos to articles to timelines to theories. Kevin's entire life since the fire spent trying to make it mean something.

Because meaningless was unbearable.

Because "your parents died for no reason" wasn't an answer a human mind could accept.

So Kevin had created meaning. Had built elaborate theories. Had found patterns in randomness because patterns were better than chaos.

Because conspiracy was better than cruelty.

Because if someone CHOSE this, if someone PLANNED this, then at least it wasn't random. At least it wasn't the universe just being indifferent and cruel.

But it was random.

It was cruelty.

And Kevin had spent seven years running from that truth.

This was different from all the others.

This wasn't loneliness. This wasn't invisibility. This wasn't family breaking apart.

This was grief turned to madness. This was the human need for meaning crashing against the chaos of random loss.

This wasn't about conspiracy theories.

This was about a son who missed his parents so much he'd rather believe the world was evil than accept that the world was indifferent.

Kevin needed the world to make SENSE. Needed there to be reasons. Explanations. Causes and effects. Patterns that could be found if you just looked hard enough.

Because "your parents died in a random house fire" wasn't an answer. It was chaos. It was cruelty. It was the universe saying "sometimes bad things happen and there's no reason and you just have to live with that."

Unbearable.

So Kevin was trying to give it meaning. Even if the meaning was dark. Even if the meaning hurt. Even if the meaning destroyed his life.

At least it was SOMETHING.

Santa's throat tightened.

He understood. God, he understood.

Because he did the same thing. Spent seventeen hundred years trying to MEAN something. Trying to matter. Trying to prove that love could push back against chaos.

Maybe it couldn't.

Maybe chaos always won in the end.

But you tried anyway.

From his bag, Santa pulled photo albums. Three of them. Heavy. Leather-bound. Old.

Saved from the fire seven years ago.

He'd been there that night. Had heard the call on the emergency frequencies he monitored (because how else would he know which children needed him most?). Had seen the fire trucks. Had sent a team of elves while firefighters saved the family.

They'd grabbed what they could before the flames consumed every-thing: Albums. Documents. Keepsakes. The physical proof that the family had existed. That love had been real.

Things that would matter later.

Things Kevin thought had burned.

But Santa had saved them. Kept them safe. Waited.

Waited for seven years.

Waiting until Kevin was ready. Until he'd grieved enough that memories wouldn't destroy him. Until he was strong enough to remember without breaking.

Tonight was that night.

Santa placed the albums on the table. Beside Kevin's conspiracy boards. On top of his latest printouts and theories and desperate searching.

Solid. Real. Heavy with the weight of actual lives actually lived.

Proof of something Kevin had forgotten:

That love had existed.

That his parents had been REAL. Not just the absence of them, the hole they'd left, the conspiracy that maybe explained their deaths.

But the presence of them. The reality of them. The love that had been true even though it ended.

He added a note. Written in his neat, old-fashioned handwriting:

Kevin - I was there that night. I saved what I could. Your parents were real. Your childhood was real. Love is real. The rest is just noise. It's time to remember the real things. -Santa

Would Kevin believe it?

Would he read it as another conspiracy? Another trick? Another piece of the puzzle that proved... something?

Or would he see it for what it was: a reminder that not everything is chaos. That some things persist. That love leaves traces that not even fire can erase.

Santa stood there for a long moment.

Looking at this young man who'd lost so much. Who'd turned his grief into anger. His loss into suspicion. His love into seven years of red string and desperate theories.

"I'm sorry," Santa whispered. His voice barely audible. "I'm so, so sorry you lost them. But they were here. They loved you. That's real. That's the only real thing. Everything else is just... noise."

He meant it.

The conspiracies were noise. The theories were noise. The seven years of searching were noise.

But the love?

The love was real.

The love was the signal under all that noise.

If Kevin could just hear it.

Then Santa left. Back out into the night. Into the cold that felt less cold than the grief in that apartment.

Five more minutes until midnight.

One more house before the clock struck twelve.

One more house before everything changed.

11:58 PM - TIMMY'S HOUSE

The last house before midnight was small.

Military base housing. Neat. Sparse in that military way—everything in its place, nothing extra, function over comfort.

A single mother and her seven-year-old son.

The boy who'd written that comment on Instagram. The boy who'd saved Christmas without knowing it.

Why would the real Santa need to prove he's real?

Santa stood in the living room, and something in his chest eased.

After Marcus's breaking family. After Danny's crushing loneliness. After Sarah's invisible exhaustion. After Kevin's consuming grief.

This was different.

This was hope. Pure. Uncomplicated. Simple.

Photos of Dad everywhere. In uniform. Proud. Strong. Away.

A countdown calendar on the fridge. Timmy had already crossed off December 24th in red crayon, and Santa could see January 15th circled in the same red with "DADDY COMES HOME!!!" written so hard the crayon had almost torn through the paper.

Twenty-one days.

Just twenty-one more days.

Mom asleep on the couch. Still dressed. Exhausted in a different way than Sarah—not from chaos, but from carrying everything alone. From being both parents. From answering "when's Daddy coming home?" every single day while wondering the same thing herself.

Timmy's photo clutched in her hand. School picture from this year. Her seven-year-old son smiling at the camera, missing two front teeth.

She'd fallen asleep holding onto him. Or maybe holding onto hope. Or maybe both.

And Timmy himself, asleep upstairs in a bedroom decorated with soldier action figures and drawings he'd made of Dad "fighting bad guys" and a map of the world with a pin stuck in where Dad was deployed and a string connecting it to their house.

So young. So innocent. So completely certain that Santa was real because of course Santa was real.

Why would anyone even ask?

How did children know that? How did they understand what adults forgot?

That real things don't need proof.

That magic doesn't need validation.

That love persists whether you believe in it or not.

Santa climbed the stairs quietly. Each step an effort. Every movement a reminder of the night. Of the breaking point. Of the 1,247 houses and the billions still to go.

But also a reminder that he was still going. Still here. Still showing up.

He stood in Timmy's doorway.

The boy slept peacefully. No doubt. No fear. No hedging his bets or covering his bases.

Just trust.

Pure, absolute, uncomplicated trust that Santa would come.

Because Santa always came.

Because that's what real things do.

And Santa felt something shift in his chest.

Not breaking. Not even opening.

Settling.

Like pieces that had been scattered all day—through panic and performance and desperate proving—finally falling back into place.

This was why.

Not for Marcus who'd called him fake. Not for the millions who'd analyzed his "rendering techniques." Not for proof or metrics or validation.

For this.

For this one child sleeping peacefully because he believed. Not blindly. Not foolishly.

But with the simple, profound wisdom of someone who understood what Santa had forgotten:

Real things don't need proof.

They just show up.

From his bag, Santa pulled an envelope.

Inside: a recording. Dad's voice. Recorded two weeks ago. Santa had called in the favor personally. Had contacted the base. Had explained (as much as he could explain to a commanding officer who was 73% sure this was a prank).

Had gotten five minutes. That's all he'd asked for. Five minutes of Dad talking to his son.

Just Dad talking. Saying he missed Timmy. Counting down the days. Promising to be home soon. Promising to play catch and read stories and be the dad he'd been before deployment.

Simple. True. Everything a seven-year-old needed to hear.

Santa placed the envelope on the nightstand. With a note:

Timmy - Thank you for reminding me what matters. You were right. The real Santa doesn't need to prove anything. He just shows up. I'll always show up. Love, Santa

Then Santa did something he almost never did.

He sat on the edge of Timmy's bed.

Just for a moment.

His body protested—knees, back, shoulders, everything screaming. But he sat anyway.

Because this mattered.

This was the moment.

The reason for everything.

The answer to the question that had plagued him all day, all week, all month as he'd watched metrics and worried about belief and posted videos trying to prove he was real.

And he whispered:

"Thank you, kid."

His voice was barely audible. Raw. Honest.

"You saved me today. You reminded me why I do this. Not for the believers. Not for the proof. Just... to show up. To be here. To see you."

He paused. Felt tears prickling his eyes—different tears than before. Not tears of exhaustion or despair.

Tears of understanding.

"I was so lost today. So desperate to prove I was real. And you—you just knew. You just understood. You reminded me that real things don't need proof. They don't need validation. They don't need metrics or comments or viral videos."

Timmy stirred slightly. Smiled in his sleep.

Whispered something that sounded like "knew you'd come."

And Santa's eyes burned.

Because that was it.

That was everything.

Knew you'd come.

Not "hoped you were real." Not "needed proof." Not "had to see evidence."

Just: knew you'd come.

Because real things show up.

Because love doesn't need validation.

Because magic persists whether or not anyone believes.

Santa's hand trembled as he touched the boy's hair gently. Just once. Just barely.

"I'll always come," he whispered. His voice breaking. "Always. Every year. Every Christmas Eve. Whether anyone believes or not. Whether anyone sees or not. Whether it's enough or not. I'll always come. I promise."

Then he stood.

Every joint protesting. Every muscle screaming. His vision swimming. His hands shaking.

But standing anyway.

Because the work wasn't done yet.

Would never be done.

But that was okay.

Because the work was the point.

Downstairs, he paused by the couch where Mom slept. Left a second envelope beside Timmy's photo:

Your son is wise beyond his years. You're doing great. January 15th is coming. Hold on. -Santa

Then out.

Back to the sleigh.

Back to Rudolph who was waiting patiently, nose glowing steady.

Back to three billion, nine hundred ninety-eight million houses still waiting.

But different now.

Changed now.

Understanding now.

12:00 AM - MIDNIGHT

The stars overhead were infinite.

Santa sat in the sleigh, looking at them. At the impossible vastness. At the beauty that persisted whether anyone saw it or not.

His body ached. His throat was raw. His hands shook.

But something had shifted.

Sitting in Timmy's room. Whispering thank you to a sleeping child. Being reminded that real things don't need proof—they just show up.

Something had fundamentally changed in his understanding.

The weight was still there.

Marcus still needed his family. Danny still needed his sister. Sarah still needed rest. Kevin still needed healing. Three billion, nine hundred ninety-eight million houses still waited.

The exhaustion was still there.

Every muscle screaming. Every joint protesting. Seventeen hundred years of Christmas Eves catching up all at once.

But it didn't feel like burden anymore.

It felt like purpose.

Not because he could fix everything. He couldn't.

Not because he could save everyone. He couldn't.

But because showing up mattered.

Marcus wouldn't wake up to perfect parents. But he'd wake up to a reminder that love had existed. That trying was possible. That was something.

Danny wouldn't wake up to five years erased. But he'd wake up to his sister's words, preserved. To the knowledge that he hadn't been alone. That was something.

Sarah wouldn't wake up to a magic solution. But she'd wake up to being seen. To her children noticing. To knowing she mattered. That was something.

Kevin wouldn't wake up to his parents alive. But he'd wake up to proof they'd lived. To memories preserved. To love documented. That was something.

Timmy would wake up to his father's voice. To the promise of January 15th. To the knowledge that someone heard his wisdom and listened.

That was something.

Not everything.

Not enough to fix the world.

But something.

And maybe—just maybe—that was the point.

Not to fix everything. Not to save everyone.

Just to show up. To see. To give what you can.

To BE love in a world that needs it desperately.

Even when it's not enough.

Especially when it's not enough.

Because love doesn't calculate. Doesn't measure. Doesn't ask "is this sufficient?"

Love just gives. Just shows up. Just persists.

Whether anyone's watching or not.

Whether anyone believes or not.

Whether it's enough or not.

Santa picked up the reins.

His hands still trembled. But they held.

"Three billion more," he said to Rudolph.

Rudolph's nose flared bright.

Let's go.

They rose into the sky.

Into the cold.

Into the work that would never end, never be finished, never be enough—

And was beautiful precisely because of that.

The northern lights danced overhead. Green and purple ribbons across infinite dark.

Somewhere a star's light was traveling. From a source long dead. Still shining. Still reaching earth.

Still beautiful.

Still REAL.

Some lights travel longer than their source lives.

Some love outlasts the lover.

Some magic transcends the magician.

And some work—the real work, the sacred work—doesn't need to be enough.

It just needs to be done.

With love.

With presence.

With showing up.

Again.

And again.

And again.

Santa flew on.

Into the silent night.

Witnessed by none.

Magnificent regardless.

The work continued.

As it always had.

As it always would.

Because that's what real things do.

They persist.

They show up.

They ARE.

Proof not required.

Faith not demanded.

Just...

Present.

Always present.

Always real.

Forever.

CHAPTER 11
"CHRISTMAS MORNING"

$\sim$

December 25th, 6:00 AM - 2:00 PM

Around the World

$\sim$

6:00 AM - MARCUS

The alarm went off at 6:00 AM sharp.

Marcus had set it for Christmas morning even though his parents never got up before eight anymore. Old habit. From when Christmas mornings meant all three of them racing downstairs together, when his dad would make hot chocolate and his mom would take too many photos, when being a family felt like breathing—effortless, automatic, right.

He reached over to silence it.

His hand knocked something off the nightstand.

A photo fluttered to the floor.

Marcus blinked. Still half in dreams. Reached down.

Picked it up.

Stared.

The beach photo. His beach photo. The one taped to his wall with scotch tape, printed on regular paper from the home printer two years ago when he'd needed to remember that his parents had been happy once.

But this wasn't a printout.

This was the original.

The actual photograph from eight years ago. The edges worn soft like someone had carried it in a wallet, held it in their hands, looked at it when they needed to remember. There was a slight curve to it, the way photos get when they live in someone's pocket, pressed against their heart.

And there was a note.

His dad's handwriting.

Marcus's hands started shaking before he finished reading the first line.

Marcus - I found this in a box in the garage last night. Couldn't sleep, went looking for the Christmas lights, found this instead. Made me remember.

The paper trembled. Marcus's whole body trembled.

Your mom and I are going to talk. Really talk.

He couldn't breathe.

I don't know if we can fix this.

The words blurred.

But we're going to try.

His chest felt too tight, like his ribs had gotten smaller, like there wasn't enough room for his heart to beat properly.

Because you deserve better than two people pretending. You deserve better than what we've been giving you.

A sound escaped Marcus's throat. Not quite a sob. Not quite a gasp. Something raw and desperate and hopeful all at once.

I'm sorry we forgot how to be happy. We're going to try to remember.

Marcus pressed the photo to his chest. His eyes were burning. His throat was closing.

They might not make it. The note said so. *I don't know if we can fix this.*

But they were TRYING.

After months of silence. Months of separate recliners and careful spacing and sleeping apart while calling it "back problems"—

They were going to TRY.

"Mom?" His voice came out strangled, broken. "Dad?"

He heard it then.

Voices downstairs.

Both of them.

In the kitchen.

Together.

Marcus froze. Listening. Barely breathing.

His dad's voice: "—and we just keep doing that? Just keep pretending everything's—"

His mom, interrupting: "No. No, we stop pretending. That's what he deserves. Truth. Not this... this performance we've been doing."

"I miss you." His dad's voice cracked. "I'm sleeping thirty feet away from you and I miss you every single night."

Silence.

Then his mom, so quiet Marcus had to strain to hear: "I miss you too."

Marcus sat on his bed, photo pressed against his racing heart, and couldn't move.

They were TALKING.

Really talking.

For the first time in months—maybe years—they were in the same room saying true things instead of safe things, messy things instead of polite things, real things instead of the careful nothing they'd been speaking for so long.

Then his dad laughed. The real laugh. Not the fake cheerful one he'd been using since the spring. The one from before. From when things were good.

And his mom laughed too.

Together.

Marcus wiped his eyes with his sleeve. Then wiped them again because they wouldn't stop filling.

"Thank you," he whispered to the empty room. To the photo. To Santa. To whoever had left this here. "Thank you thank you thank you."

He heard footsteps on the stairs.

Both of them.

Coming up together.

Marcus scrambled to sit up straighter. Wiped his face fast. But he couldn't stop smiling. His face hurt from smiling. His cheeks were wet and his eyes were red and he was smiling so hard it felt like breaking and healing at the same time.

The door opened.

His parents stood there.

Side by side.

His dad's hand on his mom's shoulder. His mom leaning into him just slightly. Just enough to matter.

Both of them with red, puffy eyes. Both of them smiling.

"Merry Christmas, buddy," his dad said.

His mom's voice came out thick, unsteady: "We need to talk to you. The three of us. About... about us. About what we're going to do."

She paused. Squeezed his dad's hand.

"Together."

Marcus nodded. Couldn't speak. His throat was too full.

But he held up the photo.

And his parents saw it.

Saw themselves. Young. In love. Happy. Real.

His mom made a sound. Covered her mouth with her free hand.

His dad's eyes filled. "I didn't know if you'd want to see us. After last night. After we finally—"

"I want to see you," Marcus managed. "I want to see you guys trying. That's all I wanted. Just... trying."

His dad crossed the room. Sat on the edge of the bed. His mom followed.

They sat together. The three of them.

Marcus's family.

Not fixed. Not healed. Not magically repaired by one conversation on Christmas morning.

But TRYING.

Choosing each other. Choosing honesty. Choosing to fight for what they'd once had instead of pretending it didn't matter.

That was enough.

That was more than enough.

That was everything.

∽

6:15 AM - DANNY

Danny woke to his alarm like he did every morning—reaching for his phone on autopilot, already composing the first lines of code in his head, already planning the work that would fill the next sixteen hours until he was tired enough to sleep again.

His hand touched paper instead of plastic.

Danny stopped.

Opened his eyes.

There was an envelope on his pillow.

Old paper. Edges yellowed like something that had been kept in a drawer for years, waiting. Careful creases like it had been folded and unfolded and folded again by hands that couldn't decide whether to keep it or throw it away.

His name on the front.

In handwriting he'd know anywhere. Would know blind. Would know if he lived to be a hundred.

Em.

Danny's hands shook as he picked it up.

For five years he'd been alone in this apartment. Five years of telling himself he preferred it this way. That isolation was safer than rejection. That being alone was a choice, not a consequence.

Five years of drafting emails he never sent.

And here, on Christmas morning, was an envelope in his sister's handwriting.

He opened it.

The paper inside was the same yellowed tone. Like it had been sitting in a drawer too. Waiting for someone brave enough to send it.

Danny - I don't know if you'll ever read this.

Three words. That's all it took. Three words and his vision blurred.

I don't know if you even want to hear from me.

Danny's hands were shaking so badly the paper rattled.

But I'm writing it anyway because if I don't, I'll regret it forever.

He had to stop reading. Had to breathe. Couldn't breathe.

I miss you.

The words hit like a fist.

I miss my brother.

Danny made a sound. Pressed his palm against his mouth to stop it.

I miss the person who taught me to code, who stayed up all night helping me with my calculus homework, who believed in me when no one else did.

He was crying now. Silent. Shaking. Tears dropping onto the yellowed paper, smudging the ink.

I don't know what happened to us. I don't know when we stopped talking. But I want to fix it.

Danny's chest hurt. Actually hurt. Like something had been compressed for five years and was finally expanding, breaking through scar tissue and fear and all the careful walls he'd built.

I want you back in my life.

"Em," he whispered.

Call me. Please.

Love, Em

The letter fell from Danny's hands onto the bed.

He stared at it.

At the words blurring together through his tears.

Then he saw the Post-It note stuck to the pillowcase. Different handwriting. Neat. Old-fashioned. The kind of careful penmanship you learned with a fountain pen, not a keyboard:

She wrote this but never sent it. She was scared you didn't want to hear from her. She was wrong. Call her. -S

Three years.

Emily had written this three years ago.

Three years he'd been sitting in this apartment thinking she'd moved on, thinking she'd decided he wasn't worth the trouble, thinking he'd burned that bridge so badly there was nothing left but ash.

Three years she'd been wherever she was—Portland, he remembered suddenly, she'd moved to Portland—thinking the exact same thing.

Three years they'd both been wrong.

Three years of loneliness that didn't need to exist.

Danny's hands fumbled for his phone. Found Emily's contact.

Her name on the screen. The photo from six years ago—before every-thing broke. Both of them at his college graduation. Her arm around his shoulders. Both of them smiling.

When had he last looked at this photo? When had he last dared to?

His thumb hovered over the call button.

What if she didn't answer?

What if three years was too long?

What if she'd written that letter and then changed her mind, decided he wasn't worth it, decided to let him go?

What if—

He pressed call before the fear could stop him.

It rang once.

Twice.

Danny's heart was beating so hard he could feel it in his throat.

Three times.

Maybe she was asleep. It was 6:15 in the morning. Maybe she didn't hear it. Maybe—

"Hello?" Emily's voice. Rough with sleep. Confused.

Danny opened his mouth.

Nothing came out.

His throat had closed completely. Five years of silence had become literal, physical, choking silence.

"Hello?" Emily said again. More awake now. "Who is this?"

Say something. Anything. Just—

"Danny?" Her voice changed. Sharp. Urgent. Scared. "Danny, is that you?"

"I got your letter," he whispered.

The words came out broken. Barely audible. But they came.

Silence on the other end.

Complete silence.

For so long Danny thought she'd hung up, that she'd heard his voice and decided no, actually, three years was long enough to change her mind—

"What letter?" Her voice was very small.

"The one you wrote three years ago. The one you didn't send. The one where you said—" His voice broke completely. He had to stop. Breathe. Try again. "Where you said you missed me."

More silence.

Then: "How did you—" A sharp inhale. "Danny, I never sent that. I threw it away. How do you HAVE that?"

"Santa," Danny said. Then laughed. A broken, slightly hysterical sound. "Santa brought it. Along with a note saying you were scared I didn't want to hear from you."

"I was scared," Emily whispered. "I am scared. Danny, I—" Her voice cracked. "I've been trying to call you for five years. I just couldn't— I thought you didn't want—"

"You IDIOT." She was crying now. He could hear it. Ragged breaths between words. "You complete and total IDIOT. I've been waiting for you to call. I thought YOU didn't want to talk to ME."

"I did. I do. I—" Danny pressed his palm against his eyes. Five years of loneliness trying to escape all at once. "I miss you. I'm so sorry. For everything. For disappearing. For letting you think I didn't—"

"Shut up," Emily said, but she was laughing through the tears. "Just shut up. Where are you?"

"Seattle."

"I'm in Portland."

"That's three hours." Danny was already standing. Already looking for his keys.

"I know."

Silence. Different from before. Not empty. Full. Heavy with five years of missing each other.

"I could drive down," Danny said. "Today. Right now."

"Danny, it's 6:15 in the morning on Christmas."

"I don't care."

More silence.

Then Emily's voice, so small and broken and hopeful it hurt to hear: "I'm making coffee. Drive safe."

The call ended.

Danny stood in his empty apartment. The apartment that had been his tomb for five years. The apartment where he'd convinced himself that isolation was safety and loneliness was peace and needing people was weakness.

Holding his phone.

Tears streaming down his face.

She wanted to see him.

She'd been WAITING.

All this time—five years of deleting emails and avoiding calls and convincing himself he was better off alone—she'd been waiting.

He wasn't alone.

He'd never been alone.

Danny started laughing. And crying. And couldn't tell which was which and didn't care.

He got dressed in the clothes piled on his chair. Grabbed his keys from the desk. His jacket from the hook.

Paused at the door.

Looked back at the apartment. At the monitors. At the code. At the life he'd built that wasn't a life at all.

"Thank you," he said to the empty room.

Then he left.

Ran down fourteen flights of stairs because he couldn't wait for the elevator.

Burst out into the cold Christmas morning.

And drove toward Portland.

Toward his sister.

Toward home.

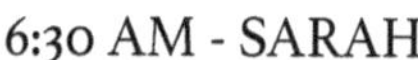

6:30 AM - SARAH

Sarah woke on the couch with a crick in her neck that suggested she'd slept at an angle that would hurt for days.

Sunlight streaming through the window. Bright. Too bright.

The vague sense that she'd forgotten something important pressing at the edges of her awareness.

Christmas.

Oh god, Christmas.

The presents weren't wrapped. The cookies weren't made. The kids' stockings were still empty and she'd meant to fill them last night but she'd just needed to sit down for one second, just one second to rest and—

Sarah sat up. Too fast. The room spun.

The kids. Were they awake? Had they come down? Had she missed Christmas morning completely?

Had she FAILED Christmas?

Her hand touched something.

A gift bag.

Red and green. Professional. The kind with tissue paper carefully arranged at the top.

Sitting on the coffee table. Right beside where her head had been.

Sarah blinked at it. Confused.

She didn't remember seeing this last night. Had the kids left it? Had her husband come down after she'd fallen asleep and—

She pulled out the tissue paper.

Inside: an envelope. Thick. Expensive paper.

North Star Spa

Full Day Package

Massage • Facial • Mani-Pedi • Aromatherapy

Recipient: Sarah Mitchell

Sarah stared at it.

This wasn't from the kids. This was... professional. Printed. Real.

Who would—

There was a note.

Sarah pulled it out with shaking hands.

Mom - We booked you a spa day. January 3rd. Dad's taking the day off. We're taking care of everything. You don't get to say no. We see you. We love you. Thank you for everything. - Your kids

The handwriting was Madison's. All four kids had signed it at the bottom. Madison's careful cursive. James's awkward print. Emma's enthusiastic bubbles over the i's. Little Michael's name spelled wrong but proud.

Sarah read it once.

The words didn't make sense.

Read it again.

We see you.

The paper started shaking.

Thank you for everything.

"Mom?"

Sarah looked up.

All four kids stood at the bottom of the stairs. Still in their Christmas pajamas. Madison in front, twelve years old and trying to look confident. James behind her, nine and anxious. Emma bouncing on her toes, seven and unable to stand still. Michael clutching his stuffed elephant, four and thumb in mouth.

Watching. Waiting.

Scared she'd be mad.

Hoping she'd understand.

"Did you—" Sarah's voice cracked. She had to clear her throat. Try again. "Did you do this?"

Madison nodded. Took a step forward. "Santa helped. He sent us a message. Told us you needed it. That you were tired. That we should help."

"I'm not—" Sarah started automatically.

Then stopped.

Because she WAS tired.

She was so tired she'd fallen asleep on the couch mid-motion. So tired she couldn't remember the last time she'd done something just for herself. So tired she'd started dreaming about running away, just getting in the car and driving until she couldn't see her life in the rearview mirror anymore.

She was tired.

And her children—her babies—they'd SEEN it.

Not just noticed. Seen. Really seen.

Seen past the "I'm fine" and the "don't worry about me" and the smile she wore like armor.

Seen the truth underneath.

"Come here," Sarah whispered.

All four kids rushed forward.

Piled onto the couch. Tangled around her. Elbows in her ribs and knees on her legs and hands in her hair and breath on her neck.

Her children.

Her whole world.

Sarah wrapped her arms around all of them. Held them so tight they squeaked.

"Thank you," she sobbed into their hair. "Thank you thank you thank you."

"You don't have to do everything alone, Mom," Madison said quietly. Her voice muffled against Sarah's shoulder. "We can help. We WANT to help."

"I know," Sarah said. "I know now. I'm sorry I didn't— I thought I had to—"

"You don't," James said matter-of-factly. "Families help each other. That's what families DO."

Sarah laughed through her tears. "You're right. You're absolutely right."

"Are you mad?" Emma asked. Small voice. Worried.

"Mad?" Sarah pulled back to look at them. At their anxious faces. At these four humans she'd somehow made, somehow kept alive, somehow raised to be thoughtful and kind and SEEING. "I'm not mad. I'm so, so grateful."

"Can we do Christmas now?" Michael asked. Thumb out of mouth. Eyes bright.

Sarah laughed again. Wiped her face. "Yes. Yes, we can do Christmas now."

They untangled themselves. Started moving toward the tree.

Sarah stayed on the couch for one more moment. Looking at the gift bag. At the spa certificate. At the note in her daughter's handwriting.

We see you.

Three words.

Three words that meant everything.

She'd been invisible for so long. Not to the world—the world had never stopped seeing her, demanding from her, taking from her.

But to herself.

She'd disappeared under the weight of MOM and WIFE and CARE-TAKER until Sarah had become just a function. A role. A list of tasks that never ended.

But her children saw her.

Really saw her.

Saw the exhaustion. Saw the sacrifice. Saw the person underneath the title.

And they'd done something about it.

Sarah pressed the note against her chest.

Then stood.

Joined her children by the tree.

Sat on the floor among the wrapping paper chaos and toy explosions and chocolate coin wrappers.

Being seen.

Being loved.

Being enough.

7:00 AM - KEVIN

Kevin woke in the chair with his neck stiff and his back screaming and the kind of disorientation that comes from falling asleep some-where you didn't mean to fall asleep.

Same as every morning for the last two years.

The conspiracy boards glowed in the morning light. Red string casting shadows on the wall like a spider web. Photos and printouts and circled connections—seven years of trying to make sense of chaos.

Kevin started to reach for his laptop. The instinct automatic. Check the forums. Read the overnight posts. Keep searching. Keep digging. Keep trying to find the pattern that would explain why the world had taken his parents.

His hand stopped.

There were photo albums on the table.

Three of them.

Leather-bound. Old. The kind with actual pages, not digital files. The kind you held in your hands.

Covering his conspiracy boards.

No—not covering. Replacing.

Sitting there like they were more important than the boards. Like they were MORE REAL than the boards.

Kevin stared at them.

Didn't touch them.

Couldn't touch them.

Because he knew what they were.

He knew without opening them.

The albums from before. From home. From the house that had burned.

The albums that had turned to ash seven years ago while he'd stood in the street with his aunt's arms around him, watching his childhood turn to smoke.

These couldn't be real.

They'd burned.

He'd WATCHED them burn.

But they were here.

On his table.

In the morning light.

Real.

Kevin's hands reached out. Trembling. Touched the top album.

The leather was cool. Worn smooth. The kind of worn that comes from being handled gently for decades. Real texture. Real weight.

So real.

His hands shook as he opened it.

His mother's face stared up at him.

Young. Smiling. In a wedding dress that had probably been in a box somewhere before the fire.

His father beside her. Looking at her like she was the only person in the world. Like nothing else existed. Like love was the only fact that mattered.

Kevin made a sound.

Not quite a sob. Not quite a gasp. Just a sound of something breaking.

Or maybe something healing.

Hard to tell the difference.

His fingers traced his mother's face. The photograph smooth under his touch. Her smile preserved. Frozen in this moment of perfect happiness. Before Kevin. Before the house. Before the fire. Before everything.

He turned the page.

Both of them holding a baby. Him. Kevin as an infant. Red-faced and screaming, probably. But his parents looking at him like he was a miracle. Like he was the best thing that had ever happened to them.

Their faces full of love. Full of hope. Full of the belief that the world was good and safe and their child would grow up happy.

They'd been wrong about safe.

But they'd been right about love.

Kevin's vision blurred. He wiped his eyes roughly. Turned another page.

His fourth birthday. Chocolate cake smashed on his face. His dad's arm around his mom. Both of them laughing at something Kevin had just said.

His eighth birthday. Running through the sprinkler in the backyard. Both parents on the porch. Watching. Waving. Present.

His thirteenth birthday. The three of them. A family. Whole. Real. HERE.

Kevin closed the album carefully.

Pressed both hands against the cover.

These had burned.

He'd WATCHED them burn.

He'd stood in the street in his aunt's borrowed jacket and watched seven years of memories turn to smoke and ash and nothing.

But someone had saved them.

Gone into the burning house—or sent someone in—and grabbed what could be grabbed. Albums. Memories. Proof that his family had existed.

Kept them safe for seven years.

Waited.

Waited until Kevin was ready. Until he'd grieved enough that seeing his parents' faces wouldn't destroy him. Until he was strong enough to remember without breaking.

He saw the note then. On a Post-It stuck to the table. Different handwriting from anything on his boards. Neat. Careful. Old-fashioned:

Kevin - I was there that night. I saved what I could. Your parents were real. Your childhood was real. Love is real. The rest is just noise. It's time to remember the real things. -Santa

Kevin read it once.

Twice.

Three times.

Love is real. The rest is just noise.

He looked at his conspiracy boards.

Seven years.

Seven years of red string and patterns and desperate searching for reasons. Seven years of trying to make tragedy make sense. Seven years of choosing chaos theory over memory. Choosing suspicion over grief. Choosing noise over truth.

Because noise was easier than silence.

Because if he could find a reason—any reason—then maybe it wouldn't hurt so much.

But there was no reason.

Sometimes houses just catch fire. Sometimes parents just die. Sometimes the world is chaos and cruelty and there's no pattern, no conspiracy, no grand design that explains why good people stop breathing.

Sometimes love just ends.

Not because of anything. Not because of reasons.

Just because.

And you either spend your life searching for reasons that don't exist.

Or you choose to remember the love that did.

Kevin stood slowly.

His legs shook. His hands shook. Everything shook.

He walked to the conspiracy boards.

Stood in front of seven years of obsession.

Then started taking them down.

Not angry. Not violent. Just... done.

He pulled down the photos of his parents' last day. The timeline he'd constructed. The supposed "evidence" of accelerant patterns. The connections he'd drawn between unrelated events.

All of it.

Pulled it down piece by piece.

The red string fell away like a web dissolving. Like something that had seemed solid revealing itself as illusion.

Seven years of searching.

And he'd been looking in the wrong direction the whole time.

His parents weren't in the patterns. Weren't in the theories. Weren't hiding in some grand conspiracy that would make their deaths mean something.

They were in the albums.

In the photos.

In the memories of birthday cakes and sprinklers and love that had been real even if it hadn't lasted.

Kevin ripped down the last photo. The last connection. The last desperate attempt to make chaos make sense.

Then stood in front of bare walls.

Breathing hard.

Crying.

Finally crying.

For the first time in seven years, crying not from anger but from grief. Real grief. The kind that doesn't demand reasons. The kind that just hurts because loss hurts and that's all there is to it.

He went back to the table.

Opened the first album again.

His mother's face smiled up at him.

Real.

Still real.

Always real.

"I'm sorry," Kevin whispered to the photo. His voice breaking. "I'm sorry I forgot. I'm sorry I let the noise get so loud I couldn't hear the real things anymore."

He touched her face gently. The photograph smooth under his fingertips.

"I'm going to remember now," he promised. "I'm going to remember the real things. I'm going to remember you were HERE. That you loved me. That was REAL. That's what matters. Not the fire. Not the why. Just... you were here. You loved me. That's real."

He opened his laptop with shaking hands.

Navigated to his conspiracy forum. Seven years of posts. Thousands of hours. An entire identity built on suspicion and doubt and desperate searching.

Hovered the mouse over the delete button.

Thought about all the people who followed him. Who believed him. Who'd joined him in the noise because it was easier than the silence.

Then thought about his mother's face. Smiling in that wedding photo. Real. True. Love that had existed whether he'd spent seven years honoring it or destroying it.

He deleted the forum.

Every post. Every theory. Seven years of wrong answers.

Gone.

In its place, he typed a new search: "grief support groups near me"

Found one. St. Mark's Community Center. Tuesdays at 7 PM.

Two days.

He could do two days.

Kevin closed the laptop.

Opened the second album.

And started remembering.

Not the fire. Not the loss. Not the chaos.

But the love.

The real things.

The only things that mattered.

∼

8:00 AM - TIMMY

"MOM! MOM! MOM!"

Timmy's voice exploded through the house like a fire alarm at full volume.

His mother jerked awake on the couch. Heart hammering. Terror flooding her system with adrenaline. The instant panic of a parent hearing their child scream.

"What? What's wrong?" She was on her feet before she was fully conscious. "Are you hurt? What happened?"

Timmy appeared at the top of the stairs.

Holding something.

His face split by the biggest smile she'd ever seen. The kind of smile that uses every muscle in the face. The kind that radiates pure, uncomplicated joy.

"SANTA CAME!"

She exhaled. Pressed her hand to her racing heart. "I know, baby. There are presents under the tree. You can come down and—"

"NO!" Timmy was bouncing. Actually bouncing. "Not toys! Better than toys! MOM, SANTA BROUGHT DAD!"

She blinked. "What?"

Timmy bounded down the stairs. Took them two at a time in a way that made her heart clench with second-hand terror. But he made it. Landed at the bottom. Rushed to her.

Shoved an envelope into her hands.

"Dad wrote me a letter! Santa brought Dad's letter! Listen!"

He was already pulling out a small recording device. Digital voice recorder. The kind deployed parents used to send messages home.

Pressed play.

Her husband's voice filled the room.

Warm. Real. Alive.

Hey buddy. It's Dad.

Timmy's mother's hands flew to her mouth.

I'm recording this because Santa said you might need to hear my voice. And also because I need to say this stuff out loud. Make it real.

She sank onto the couch. Legs giving out.

I miss you so much, kiddo. I miss you and Mom more than anything in the world. I know I said that in my last email, but I need you to really hear it. Every day here is just... it's just time I'm not with you guys. And that's hard. That's really hard.

Timmy was vibrating with excitement beside her. Bouncing on his toes. Unable to contain himself.

But I'm coming home soon. January 15th. That's twenty-one days from when Santa said he'd deliver this. Twenty-one days. I'm counting every single one.

Her throat closed completely. Tears spilling over.

And when I get home, we're going to do ALL the things. We're going to play catch in the backyard even though it'll be January and probably freezing. We're going to build the LEGO Death Star you've been asking for. We're going to read Harry Potter together—your pick which book we start with. We're going to make pancakes on Saturday mornings and let Mom sleep in because she's the one holding down the fort while I'm gone and she deserves it.

Timmy grabbed her hand. Squeezed it tight.

I'm going to be the dad I was before I left. Before deployment. Before all of this. I'm going to be present. I'm going to be THERE. Not just physically. Really there.

Her husband's voice wavered. Got thick.

I promise, buddy. January 15th. I'm coming home. I love you more than the whole universe. Tell Mom I love her too. So much. Tell her to hang on. I'm almost there.

Love, Dad

The recording ended.

Silence.

Then Timmy: "Twenty-one days, Mom!"

He ran to the kitchen. She heard him crossing off the calendar.

"No, wait—" Rustling paper. "Today's the 25th so that's—TWENTY days! Mom, Dad's coming home in TWENTY DAYS!"

His mother sat on the couch.

Holding the recorder.

Crying.

Not sad crying. Not scared crying.

The kind of crying that happens when hope becomes real instead of theoretical. When the abstract idea of "he's coming home" becomes a voice you can hear, a promise you can hold, a countdown you can believe.

Twenty days.

She could do twenty days.

They'd already done 247 days. Another twenty was nothing.

"Mom?" Timmy appeared in the doorway. Stopped bouncing. Concerned. "Why are you sad?"

"I'm not sad, baby." She wiped her face. Smiled at him through tears. "I'm happy. I'm so, so happy."

"Because Dad's coming home?"

"Because Dad's coming home. And because Santa saw you."

"I knew he would." Timmy said it matter-of-factly. With absolute certainty. "I told everyone on the internet. The real Santa doesn't need to prove anything. He just shows up."

He climbed onto the couch beside her. Leaned against her side.

"And he DID show up. Just like I said."

His mother wrapped her arm around him. Pulled him close.

"He did. You were right."

They sat together in the Christmas morning light. The recorder between them. Evidence of love reaching across distance. Proof that some promises persist even when everything else falls apart.

"Can we listen to it again?" Timmy asked.

"Yes. As many times as you want."

He pressed play.

His father's voice filled the room again.

Hey buddy. It's Dad...

They listened.

And counted down.

Twenty days.

9:00 AM - THE INTERNET EXPLODES

Marcus posted first.

His hands shook as he typed it out. Sitting at the kitchen table while his parents made breakfast together. Actually together. His mom chopping fruit while his dad scrambled eggs and they talked—really talked—about couples therapy and what they'd both been afraid to say and how they'd gotten so lost.

He took a photo. His parents. In the kitchen. His dad's hand on his mom's shoulder. Both of them smiling.

Uploaded it to Instagram.

Caption: *@NaughtyOrNice I don't understand how you knew. I don't understand when you came to my house. But my parents are in the kitchen right now planning their vow renewal for April. You gave me my family back. I don't have words for what that means. Thank you doesn't cover it. But thank you.*

Posted.

Put the phone down.

Picked it up thirty seconds later to 400 likes.

By the time his mom brought him breakfast, it was at 7,000.

Danny posted from a rest stop outside Portland.

Pulled over because his hands were shaking too badly to drive.

Photo of Emily's letter spread across his steering wheel. The yellowed paper. The words. The proof that he hadn't been alone.

Caption: *@NaughtyOrNice I'm driving to Portland right now to see my sister for the first time in 5 years. You saved a letter she wrote but never sent three years ago. How did you HAVE that? How did you KNOW? I don't understand any of this. But I'm thirty minutes from seeing her and I can't stop crying and I just wanted to say thank you. You gave me my sister back.*

Posted.

12,000 likes in twenty minutes.

Then 18,000.

Then 25,000.

Comments flooding in:

how did Santa have a letter your sister never sent

this is actually impossible

ok I'm starting to believe

WAIT HOW DID HE KNOW

~

Sarah posted from her couch. Surrounded by her children. Toy chaos everywhere. Breakfast forgotten.

She took a photo of the note. All four signatures. Madison's careful handwriting. *We see you.*

Caption: *To all the exhausted parents who think nobody notices: Someone notices. Your kids notice. You're not invisible. You're not failing. You're doing MORE than enough. Someone sees you. I promise.*

She tagged @MomOf4KidsNoSleep to her own username so people could find her real account.

Posted.

The response was immediate.

In the first hour: 112,000 likes.

Comments from mothers she'd never met:

I needed to see this today

I'm crying at my kitchen table

how did you know I needed this

I'm so tired and this made me feel seen

thank you thank you thank you

Sarah sat there watching the comments flood in. Watching hundreds of thousands of exhausted mothers finding each other. Seeing each other. Saying "me too" and "you're not alone" and "I see you."

Not because of Santa.

Because of each other.

Santa had seen her first.

But now they were seeing each other.

Kevin posted at 9:47 AM. Right before he deleted his forum.

Final post on @TruthSeeker2031.

Photo of the wedding album. His parents smiling. Real. True. Love that had existed.

Caption: *I've spent seven years telling you nothing is real. That everything is fake. That you can't trust anything or anyone. That the world is chaos and conspiracy and nothing means what it seems to mean. I was wrong. I was so, so wrong. Love is real. Memory is real. This photo in my hands is REAL. Someone saved it from a fire seven years ago. Kept it safe. Waited until I was ready to remember instead of rage. That's not conspiracy. That's love. I'm shutting down the forum. Not because I've been silenced. Because I've been wrong. Thank you for listening to me. But I have to go. I have a life to live. I have memories to honor. I have real things to remember.*

He attached a photo of his bare walls. The conspiracy boards gone.

Posted.

Watched the forum watch him in real-time.

15,000 people online. All of them seeing his final message.

Comments started immediately:

wait what

Kevin are you okay

what happened

did someone get to you

KEVIN

But also:

I'm happy for you man

this is beautiful

I lost my mom last year and I've been doing the same thing maybe we've all been looking in the wrong direction

love is real

thank you for this

At 9:47 AM, Kevin deleted the forum.

Seven years of conspiracies.

Gone.

Replaced with one photo of his parents smiling on their wedding day.

Real things.

Under Santa's last post—the one that just said "Believe or don't. Either way, I have work to do."—the shift was visible.

Like watching a tide change.

Before Christmas morning, the comments had been:

fake

CGI

AI-generated

nice try

Amazon LED for $12.99

this is obviously rendered

where's the proof

After Christmas morning:

how did you know about my parents

this is exactly what I needed

you SAW me

I don't understand how you KNEW

what kind of technology can do this

this isn't possible

you were in my house

HOW DID YOU KNOW

The question changing.

Not "is he real?"

But "HOW?"

Tech experts weighing in:

I've analyzed the chimney footage frame by frame. If this is CGI, it's using rendering technology that doesn't exist yet. The physics are perfect. The reindeer breathing. The snow displacement. I can't find the fake.

I'm a senior animator at Pixar. This level of detail would take a team of 50 people six months to render. He posted it in real-time. Someone explain.

The photogrammetry alone would require equipment he couldn't fit in a sleigh. I don't understand what I'm looking at.

But more than the tech experts, regular people:

He knew my grandmother died

He left my mom's favorite flowers

He brought me a photo I thought was lost

He knew my daughter's name

He knew what we needed

He KNEW

By 10:00 AM, the sentiment analysis had shifted from 73% skeptical to 51% believing.

By 11:00 AM, it was 60%.

Not because of proof.

Because of stories.

Because of people sharing what they'd found Christmas morning. What had been left. What had been known. What had been seen.

Hundreds of stories.

Thousands of stories.

Tens of thousands.

All over the world, people waking up to discover they'd been SEEN.

That Santa—or someone, or something—had known what they needed. Had cared. Had helped.

And underneath all those stories, a new conversation emerging:

Maybe proof doesn't matter

Maybe it's not about whether he's real

Maybe it's about what he gave us

Look at all these people connecting

Look at all these people being seen

That's the real magic

11:00 AM - NORTH POLE

Jinglebert stood in the control room, staring at his tablet.

The metrics were exploding.

127 million views on the chimney video.

89 million likes on the "Believe or don't" post.

The sentiment analysis climbing by the minute.

But that wasn't what had him frozen.

It was the comments.

The stories.

The QUANTITY of stories.

He'd tracked five people specifically. The five on Santa's route that he'd flagged as important.

But there were more.

So many more.

Hundreds. Thousands. Tens of thousands.

People sharing what they'd found. What had been left. How Santa had known.

A woman in Brazil: *He left me my grandfather's watch. I thought it was stolen. How did he HAVE it?*

A man in India: *He knew my son was sick. Left a note with a doctor's name. That doctor saved my son's life.*

A teenager in Germany: *He knew I was trans before I told anyone. Left me a book about coming out. I've never felt so seen.*

On and on and on.

All over the world.

People being SEEN.

"Jinglebert?"

He jumped.

Mrs. Claus stood in the doorway. Covered in flour. A knowing smile on her face.

"Is he still asleep?"

"Yes, ma'am. Out cold. Hasn't checked his phone."

"Good. Let him rest. He's earned it."

She walked over. Looked at the tablet screen. At the numbers. At the stories flooding in.

"How many?" she asked.

"I don't know. Tens of thousands. Maybe hundreds of thousands. I'm still trying to track them all."

"You can't," she said gently. "There are too many. There have always been too many. Kris touches so many lives. Most of them never share. Never post. Never tell anyone. They just... carry it forward."

Jinglebert was quiet for a moment.

"Did we do the right thing?" he asked. "All of this? The social media. The stress. The panic. The breaking point yesterday where I thought he was going to—"

"Yes," Mrs. Claus said firmly. "Because he learned. And they learned. Sometimes the hard path is the only path that teaches what needs teaching."

"What did they learn?"

She walked to the window. Looked out at the reindeer grazing in the snow. At Rudolph standing apart, nose still glowing faintly even in daylight. Looking toward the house. Waiting.

"That love leaves traces," she said. "That being seen matters more than being believed. That showing up is magic enough."

Jinglebert pulled up the sentiment analysis again.

"73% didn't believe yesterday. Now it's 60% DO believe. The shift is remarkable."

"And what does Kris say about that?"

"He doesn't know yet. He's still asleep."

"When he wakes up, what do you think he'll say?"

Jinglebert thought about it. About the man who'd wanted so desperately to be believed yesterday. Who'd posted the chimney video thinking proof would matter. Who'd broken down at 11:34 PM under the weight of three billion homes.

Who'd sat in Timmy's room and learned that real things don't need proof.

"I think," Jinglebert said slowly, "he'll say the numbers don't matter. That the work matters. That showing up matters. That the metrics are just... noise."

Mrs. Claus smiled. "Then he really did learn."

She turned back toward the kitchen. "I'm making cookies. Extra chocolate chip. For when he wakes up. Want to help?"

Jinglebert looked at his tablet one more time.

At the numbers still climbing.

At the comments still flooding in.

At the world waking up to magic.

Then he powered it off.

"Yes, ma'am. I'd love to help."

They walked to the kitchen together. Leaving the metrics behind.

The numbers would still be there tomorrow.

But today?

Today there were cookies to make.

And a hero to celebrate.

And a lesson to remember:

The work is the point.

Not the applause.

∼

12:30 PM - SANTA WAKES

Afternoon light.

Golden. Warm. The specific quality of Christmas afternoon when everything feels slower, softer, like the world itself is taking a breath.

Coffee waiting beside the bed. Still hot.

Magic? Martha's timing? Both?

Santa stretched slowly. Every muscle screamed. Every joint protested. Seventeen hundred years old and Christmas still kicked his ass.

Worth it though.

Always worth it.

He smiled at that thought. Reached for the coffee. Took a sip.

Perfect.

Like everything Martha did.

Then hesitated. His phone sat on the nightstand. Screen dark. Waiting.

Did he want to know?

Did it matter?

He remembered yesterday's panic. The desperate need to be believed. The metrics obsession. The breaking point at 11:34 PM when his body gave out under the weight of trying to prove he was real.

He remembered Timmy's words, scrolling past on Instagram: *The real Santa doesn't need to prove anything. He just shows up.*

He'd shown up.

Done the work.

Whether they believed or not...

He'd shown up.

Santa picked up the phone. Unlocked it.

128 million views.

The number didn't register at first.

That couldn't be right.

He blinked. Refreshed.

129 million.

"Martha?" His voice was rough with sleep.

"In the kitchen, dear!"

He got up slowly. Every step an effort. Every movement a reminder of last night. But he made it.

Walked to the kitchen.

Mrs. Claus looked up from her mixing bowl. Flour on her nose. A smile on her face.

"Good afternoon, sleepyhead."

"Martha, the video has—"

"I know."

"And the post has—"

"I know."

He stared at her. "Did you look?"

"Jinglebert kept me updated. But I didn't want to wake you."

Santa looked at the phone again. Started scrolling through comments.

Not the "fake" ones.

The "how did you know" ones.

The "you saw me" ones.

The "thank you" ones.

He stopped on Marcus's post. Read it. Read it again.

You gave me my family back.

"They're not talking about whether I'm real anymore," Santa said quietly.

Mrs. Claus came to stand beside him. Wiped her hands on her apron. Looked at the screen.

"What do you mean?"

"Look." He scrolled slowly. Showed her. "They're not asking 'is he real.' They're asking 'how did he know.' They're sharing stories. Connecting. Supporting each other."

He kept scrolling.

Person after person sharing what they'd found. What had been left. What had been known.

But more than that—people responding to EACH OTHER.

I'm so happy for you

You're not alone

I understand what you're going through

Here's what helped me

We're all in this together

"They're seeing each other," Santa whispered.

Mrs. Claus smiled. "Isn't that better?"

Santa was quiet for a long time. Just scrolling. Reading. Watching the conversation unfold.

Not about him.

About each other.

He found @SantaClausReal_Official2's comment buried in the thread:

You're the real deal. I'm just a guy in a suit trying to make sick kids smile at the mall. But you? You're THE Santa. Keep doing what you do. P.S. - The hospital where I volunteer offered me a full-time position working with terminal kids. Starting January. Thank you for the inspiration.

Santa's voice broke. "He wasn't competing. He was serving."

"Like you," Mrs. Claus said gently.

"I almost hated him. Yesterday. When I saw him getting more likes than my chimney video. I almost—"

"But you didn't."

"No. I didn't."

He kept scrolling. Found Danny's post about driving to Portland. Found Sarah's post about being seen. Found Kevin's final post before deleting his forum.

Love is real. The rest is just noise.

Santa set the phone down carefully on the counter.

Looked at his wife.

"I wanted them to believe in me."

"And?"

"But they didn't need to believe in ME. They needed to believe in LOVE. In being known. In mattering. In not being alone."

"Yes."

"The magic was never about proving I could fly."

"No."

"Never about the workshop or the reindeer or the deliveries."

"No."

"It was always about the SEEING. The caring. The showing up. The knowing what someone needed and giving it even when they didn't ask. Even when they didn't know they needed it."

"Yes."

Santa was quiet for a moment. Looking out the kitchen window. At the reindeer grazing in the afternoon light. At Rudolph's nose glowing faintly even in daylight.

"I almost lost that yesterday. Almost forgot what mattered."

"But you remembered."

"Because of Timmy. Because of a seven-year-old who understood what I'd forgotten."

He picked up the phone again. Looked at the numbers one more time.

129 million views.

92 million likes.

Sentiment analysis: 62% believing.

He closed the app.

Set it down.

"They still don't all believe," he said.

"Does that matter?"

Santa thought about it. Really thought.

About Marcus's parents trying. About Danny driving to Portland. About Sarah being seen by her children. About Kevin choosing memory over conspiracy. About Timmy counting down twenty days.

About all of it happening whether people believed or not.

"No," he said finally. "It doesn't matter."

"Why not?"

"Because the work is real. The love is real. The seeing is real. Whether they believe in Santa or not... people are being SEEN. People are connecting. People are choosing love over loneliness, memory over noise, truth over proof."

"And that's enough?"

Santa smiled. Actually smiled. For the first time since waking up.

"That's more than enough. That's everything."

Mrs. Claus kissed his cheek. "Good. Now come help me with these cookies. Jinglebert deserves chocolate chip after yesterday."

"He does. He really does."

Santa washed his hands. Joined his wife at the counter.

Outside, the northern lights were starting even though it was only afternoon. Green ribbons dancing against blue December sky. Beautiful whether anyone was watching or not. Real whether anyone believed or not.

Just like Santa.

Just like love.

Just like magic.

1:00 PM - THE BARN

After cookies, Santa walked to the barn.

He needed to check on them. On the ones who'd carried him through the night. Who'd flown billions of miles while he'd wrestled with questions that didn't matter.

The barn was warm. Quiet. Peaceful.

The reindeer looked up as he entered. Dasher and Dancer closest. Prancer and Vixen by the hay. Comet and Cupid near the water. Donner and Blitzen in the corner, as always, together.

And Rudolph.

Standing apart.

Nose still glowing. Faintly. That ever-present light that had guided them through storms for seventeen hundred years.

Santa walked to him slowly. His legs still protesting. His back still aching. But walking anyway.

Rudolph looked at him. Those ancient eyes. That knowing expression.

You okay?

"Yeah," Santa said. "I'm okay."

You figured it out.

"I did. Thanks to a seven-year-old."

Rudolph snorted softly. *The young ones usually understand better. They haven't learned to complicate things yet.*

Santa reached out. Stroked Rudolph's neck. The fur soft under his hand. Warm. Real.

"I'm sorry about Marcus," Santa said quietly. "What he said about you. The 'Amazon LED' comment. That wasn't fair."

Rudolph was quiet for a moment.

Then: *Do you know what Marcus woke up to this morning?*

"His parents trying."

Do you know what he posted about that?

"That I gave him his family back."

And do you think he's still worried about whether my nose is real?

Santa stopped. Looked at Rudolph. At that glowing red nose that had guided them through impossible storms and impossible nights.

"No. He's not thinking about that at all."

Because the work mattered more than the criticism. The love mattered more than the doubt. The showing up mattered more than the proving.

"You knew that already."

I've known it for seventeen hundred years. But you needed to learn it again.

Santa leaned his forehead against Rudolph's neck. Closed his eyes.

"Thank you for carrying me last night. For getting me through it. For believing in the work even when I forgot why we do it."

That's what we're here for. All of us. To carry you when you need carrying. To remind you when you forget. To show up beside you, year after year, whether anyone believes or not.

Rudolph paused.

Besides, my nose IS an Amazon LED special. I get them in bulk. Very economical.

Santa laughed. Actually laughed.

Pulled back to look at Rudolph.

The reindeer's eyes were twinkling.

Made you laugh.

"You did."

Good. You needed that.

Santa stroked Rudolph's neck one more time. Then moved down the line. Greeting each reindeer. Thanking each one. Checking on them. Making sure they were okay after the night.

They were all okay.

Tired. But okay.

Ready to do it again next year.

Always ready.

Because that's what real things do.

They show up.

They persist.

They don't need proof.

They just ARE.

~

2:00 PM - THE WORKSHOP

Santa found Jinglebert in the control room. Tablet powered off. Just sitting there. Looking at the blank screen.

"Hey," Santa said.

Jinglebert jumped. "Oh! Sir! I didn't hear you come in!"

"Call me Kris."

"Right. Kris. Of course. I just— after yesterday I thought—"

"Yesterday was hard," Santa said. "For both of us."

Jinglebert nodded. Set down the tablet.

"I'm sorry," he said quietly. "About pushing the social media. About the stress. About—"

"Don't be sorry."

"But you almost—"

"I almost broke. I know. But I didn't. And I learned something I needed to learn."

"What's that?"

Santa pulled up a chair. Sat down beside the young elf. Looked at him.

"That metrics don't measure what matters. That proof doesn't create belief. That showing up is the only magic that counts."

Jinglebert was quiet for a moment.

"The numbers are still climbing," he said. "I turned off the tablet but they're still—"

"I know. I saw."

"Does it feel good? To be believed?"

Santa thought about it.

"You know what feels good? Marcus's parents talking. Danny driving to Portland. Sarah being seen by her children. Kevin choosing memory over conspiracy. Timmy counting down twenty days."

He paused.

"That feels good. The numbers are just... numbers."

Jinglebert smiled. Small. Genuine.

"Mrs. Claus said you'd say that."

"She's usually right."

"She is."

They sat together in the quiet control room. The tablet dark. The metrics forgotten.

Outside, the northern lights continued their dance.

"Same time next year?" Jinglebert asked.

Santa smiled. "Same time next year. But maybe... less panic about the metrics?"

"Definitely less panic about the metrics."

"Good."

Santa stood. Walked to the door. Stopped.

"Jinglebert?"

"Yes?"

"Thank you. For caring. For trying. For wanting people to see what we do."

"You're welcome."

"But next year?"

"Yes?"

"Let's just focus on the work. The rest will take care of itself."

"The rest will take care of itself," Jinglebert repeated. "I like that."

Santa left him there. Walked back through the workshop. Past the elves cleaning up from the night. Past the wrapping station. Past the toy assembly lines.

All of it quiet now. Peaceful. Resting.

Until next year.

When they'd do it all again.

Because that's what real things do.

They persist.

They show up.

They love.

Whether anyone's watching or not.

Whether anyone believes or not.

Whether it's enough or not.

The work continues.

Always.

LATER THAT EVENING

Santa and Mrs. Claus sat together in their living room. Fire crackling.

Hot chocolate in their hands. The kind of peaceful quiet that only comes after work well done.

"Do you want to read the comments?" she asked.

"No."

"Are you sure?"

"I'm sure."

She smiled. Sipped her chocolate.

"I'm proud of you."

"For what?"

"For learning. For remembering. For not letting the noise drown out the real things."

Santa set down his mug. Took her hand.

"I couldn't do this without you."

"I know."

"You keep me grounded."

"Someone has to."

"You remind me what matters."

"That's what love does."

They sat together. Holding hands. Watching the fire.

Somewhere in Seattle, Marcus was eating dinner with both his parents. At the same table. Really together.

Somewhere in Portland, Danny and Emily were crying and laughing and five years of silence were dissolving with every word.

Somewhere in her living room, Sarah was playing board games with her children while they planned her spa day.

Somewhere with photo albums open, Kevin was crying healing tears and remembering real things.

Somewhere in a military family's small house, Timmy was listening to his father's voice for the hundredth time and counting down twenty days.

All of it happening.

All of it real.

All of it because someone had seen them first.

Not because Santa proved he was real.

Because he showed up anyway.

"Same time next year?" Mrs. Claus asked.

Santa smiled. "Same time next year."

The northern lights danced on.

The fire crackled.

The work was done.

Until next year.

When it would continue.

As it always had.

As it always would.

Because that's what real things do.

They persist.

They show up.

They ARE.

Proof not required.

Faith not demanded.

Just...

Present.

Always present.

Always real.

Forever.

CHAPTER 12
"THE BELIEVERS"

~

December 26th, 2:00 PM - The Video

Santa stood at his office window, coffee in hand, watching the reindeer.

They grazed in the snow, peaceful, content. Rudolph stood slightly apart from the others—not isolated, just... himself. His nose glowed softly in the afternoon light, a gentle pulse like a heartbeat.

Their eyes met across the distance.

Rudolph nodded once.

You good?

Santa nodded back.

I'm good.

Behind him, his phone sat on the desk. Silent. He hadn't checked it since this morning. Hadn't felt the pull. The desperate need to know what they were saying, what they were thinking, whether they believed.

It was the strangest feeling.

Like setting down a weight he'd been carrying so long he'd forgotten it was there.

His shoulders felt lighter. His chest felt open. His breath came easier.

He'd done the work.

Shown up.

Seen people who needed to be seen.

Whether they believed him or not...

The work was done.

"Santa?"

He turned. Jinglebert stood in the doorway, tablet in hand, bouncing slightly on his toes. That nervous energy of someone with an idea they weren't sure would be welcomed.

"What is it, Jinglebert?"

"I, um. I had a thought. About the comments. About the people asking 'how did you know?' and 'how is this possible?' and—" He stopped. Took a breath. "I want to show them. Not to prove you're real. But to show them the WORK. The actual work that went into knowing."

Santa tilted his head. "What do you mean?"

"The evidence," Jinglebert said. He was talking faster now, excited. "Timmy's dad's recording. Emily's letter. Kevin's albums. The photo Marcus's parents took. I want to show people where they came from. How long it took to find them. The actual PROCESS of caring enough to save these things."

Santa was quiet for a moment.

"Why?" he asked gently.

"Because they need to understand. Not that you're magic—though you are. But that love leaves TRACES. That caring leaves evidence. That when you pay attention, when you really SEE people, there's always a trail. Always something saved. Always..." Jinglebert's voice got quieter. "Always proof that someone cared."

Santa looked at this young elf. 147 years old. Just yesterday pushing metrics and engagement and viral potential.

Today pushing something else.

Truth.

Connection.

The evidence of love.

"Show me what you have in mind," Santa said.

2:15 PM - JINGLEBERT'S WORK

They stood in the archives. Row after row of filing cabinets, boxes, hard drives, physical media from seventeen hundred years of Christmas.

"Every gift leaves a trail," Jinglebert said. He was in his element now, moving between stations, pulling up files. "Some are easy to trace. Some take... longer."

He pulled up the first file.

"Timmy's dad. Military database. Standard protocol for deployed service members—they can record messages for family. The system archives them automatically. I accessed it through our Department of Defense liaison—"

"We have a Department of Defense liaison?"

"You established the connection in 1943. Operation Christmas Drop. They never cancelled the access." Jinglebert grinned. "Anyway. Found the father's records, located the most recent message recording, pulled it. Time elapsed: fifteen minutes."

He moved to the next station.

"Emily's letter. This one was harder. Digital archaeology. Her trash folder from three years ago—but trash gets permanently deleted after thirty days, so I had to access backup systems. Google keeps rolling backups for premium accounts, which she has. Had to cross-reference dates, version histories, recover multiple deleted drafts. Like excavating layers. Each draft a little different. Some angrier. Some sadder. This one—the one we used—was the rawest. The most honest." He looked at Santa. "Time elapsed: three hours."

"Three hours," Santa repeated softly.

"For one letter. But it was worth it. She needed to know she'd tried. He needed to know she'd wanted to reach out."

Jinglebert moved again.

"Ohio Santa—Frank. Public records. Hospital volunteer logs. Twelve years of documented visits. Simple search, clear trail. He's been showing up every Tuesday and Thursday for over a decade. Never missed a week except when his own father was dying." Jinglebert's voice got thick. "Even then, he was back the next week. Kids asked where he'd been. He told them the truth: 'My dad needed me. But I'm back now. I'll always come back.' Time elapsed: twenty minutes."

Santa had to look away. His eyes were burning.

"Kevin's photos. Fire department archives. I had to request physical access—they're not digitized yet. Box in the basement of Station 7, labeled 'Henderson Fire, 2017.' Dusty. Forgotten. But preserved. They save everything from major residential fires. Evidence, they call it. But also..." Jinglebert's voice cracked slightly. "Also because someone might come back looking. Someone might need to remember. Time elapsed: forty-five minutes to find the box, photograph the contents, and restore them."

He pulled up the final file. Took a breath.

"Marcus's parents' photo. This one..." He shook his head. "This one was HARD. Pre-digital archives. Physical photo from 2003. In a box labeled 'Memory Saves 2003.' But Santa, we have thousands of boxes. THOUSANDS. I spent eight hours going through them. Manually. One box at a time. Each one full of photographs, letters, drawings— things you've saved over the years when you thought someone might need them later."

"Eight hours," Santa whispered.

"Eight hours for one photo. But when I found it..." Jinglebert turned the screen. The photo filled it. Young parents. Beach. Love. "When I found it, I understood. You saved this because you KNEW. Somehow you knew this family would need to remember. That this exact moment would matter years later. That this evidence of their love would be the thing that brought them back."

Santa couldn't speak.

"Total time," Jinglebert said. "Approximately twelve hours and twenty minutes of work across five days. But wildly uneven. Some miracles took fifteen minutes. Some took eight hours. You never know which until you start digging."

He looked at Santa.

"THAT'S what I want to show them. Not that you're magic. That LOVE is work. That caring takes time. That some people are easy to help and some require years of searching. But you do both. You've always done both. Because love doesn't calculate fair."

Santa walked to the window. Looked out at the snow. At the world that had doubted him yesterday and was starting to believe today.

"Make the video," he said quietly.

"Really?"

"Really. Show them the work. Show them the evidence. Show them that love leaves traces—if you know where to look."

2:45 PM - CREATING THE VIDEO

Jinglebert worked quickly. Not because he was rushing. Because he knew exactly what needed to be shown.

The video was raw. Unpolished. Shot on his phone.

It showed:

The computer screen. Database searches. Files opening. Timestamps visible.

TIMMY'S DAD - 15 MINUTES

Database: U.S. Military Family Messaging System

Search: [Name] [Unit] [Recording Date]

Result: Found. Message dated December 10th, 2025

Time: 6:47 PM to 7:02 PM

The boxes in the fire station basement. Jinglebert's hands dusty, opening one after another.

KEVIN'S PHOTOS - 45 MINUTES

Fire Station 7 - Evidence Archive

Henderson Fire, 2017

Box 47 of 89 from that year

Found: Photo albums, salvaged documents, personal effects

Time: 4:15 PM to 5:00 PM

The backup system interface. Lines of code. Deleted drafts recovering one by one.

EMILY'S LETTER - 3 HOURS

Google Workspace Backup Recovery

User: Emily [Last Name]

Deleted Items: November 2022

17 drafts recovered, analyzed, selected

Time: 2:30 PM to 5:30 PM

And finally—the longest sequence—Jinglebert opening box after box after box in a massive storage room.

MARCUS'S PHOTO - 8 HOURS

Physical Archives: Memory Saves 2003

Box 1: Opened. Not found.

Box 2: Opened. Not found.

Box 3: Opened. Not found.

[Time lapse showing dozens of boxes]

Box 47: FOUND

Young couple. Beach. Love.

Time: 9:00 AM to 5:00 PM

The video showed every box. The tedium. The dust. The searching. The moment of discovery when Jinglebert held up the photo, checked it against the reference image, and whispered "Got it."

Eight hours compressed into two minutes.

But those two minutes showed everything.

The work wasn't equal. The effort wasn't fair. Some saves took minutes. Some took days.

But they were all done.

All given the same care.

All treated as if they mattered completely.

Because they did.

The video ended with a simple title card:

Love leaves traces.

You just have to know where to look.

And care enough to search.

∼

3:30 PM - THE POSTING

Jinglebert held his tablet, finger hovering over the upload button.

"Are you sure?" he asked Santa.

Santa nodded. "I'm sure."

"No caption? No explanation?"

"Just the heart," Santa said. "Let the work speak for itself."

Jinglebert uploaded the video to Instagram. To the @NaughtyOrNice account that had been dark since Christmas Eve.

Posted at 3:47 PM.

Caption: 🤍

That was all.

Just a heart.

The video went live.

Within seconds: 10,000 views.

One minute: 50,000 views.

Five minutes: 500,000 views.

And the comments started loading.

But Santa didn't watch them load.

He was back at the window. Looking at the reindeer. At Rudolph's steady glow.

"Aren't you going to see what they say?" Jinglebert asked.

Santa shook his head. "Tomorrow. Maybe. But today?" He turned to look at the young elf. "Today I'm going to sit with my wife. Eat cookies. Tell her about the delivery. About Marcus and Danny and Sarah and Kevin and Timmy. About all the ones who needed to be seen."

"But the video—"

"Will be there tomorrow. The comments will be there tomorrow. The world will be there tomorrow." Santa smiled. "But right now, I'm here. With the people who matter. Doing the real work of rest."

Jinglebert looked at his tablet. At the numbers climbing. At the comments flooding in faster than he could read them.

Then he powered it off.

"Can I... can I have cookies too?"

Santa laughed. "Of course. Come on."

They walked to the kitchen together. Left the metrics behind. Left the engagement rates. Left the viral potential and the trending topics and all of it.

Because the work was done.

And rest was work too.

3:50 PM - THE KITCHEN

Mrs. Claus had made cocoa. Real cocoa, the kind that took thirty minutes and three types of chocolate and made the whole workshop smell like Christmas.

Santa sat at the table. Jinglebert beside him. Torbin had wandered in from the workshop, still covered in sawdust. Buttons emerged from the ovens, flour in her hair. Greta came down from the stables, smelling like reindeer and hay.

They sat together. The team. The family.

And Santa told them stories.

About the Japanese mother and daughter who shared a bed for warmth.

About Marcus's parents and the photo that reminded them.

About Danny driving to Portland with tears streaming down his face.

About Sarah being held by her children who finally saw her.

About Kevin taking down his conspiracy boards and opening albums instead.

About Timmy counting down twenty days with absolute faith.

"Four billion homes," Torbin said quietly. "And you remember these ones."

"I remember all of them," Santa said. "Every single one. But these..." He smiled. "These ones needed remembering. Needed someone to hold their stories. To witness them."

"You witnessed them," Mrs. Claus said. She put her hand over his. "You SAW them. That's the gift. Not the toys. The seeing."

Santa nodded. Couldn't speak for a moment.

"I almost forgot that," he said finally. "This week, I almost forgot what mattered. Thought it was belief. Thought it was proof. Thought it was—"

"Validation," Jinglebert supplied quietly.

"Yes. Validation. I wanted strangers to tell me I mattered. To tell me I was real. To tell me..." He stopped. "To tell me I was enough."

The kitchen was silent.

"But you were always enough," Mrs. Claus said gently. "You've always been enough. The work was always enough. You just forgot for a minute."

"A long minute."

"But you remembered. That's what matters."

Santa looked around the table. At these people—these beings—who'd stood by him through his doubt. Through his panic. Through his desperate need to be seen.

Who'd seen him all along.

"Thank you," he said. "For not giving up on me. For reminding me. For—"

"For loving you?" Mrs. Claus interrupted. "Kris, that's not something we have to TRY to do. That's just... who we are."

She squeezed his hand.

"You're stuck with us. Forever. Whether you believe you're worthy of it or not."

Santa laughed. Actually laughed. Full and real and from his belly.

"I guess I am."

"You ARE," Buttons said firmly. "Now eat your cookie before it gets cold."

"Cookies don't get cold, they get stale—"

"EAT THE COOKIE, SANTA."

He ate the cookie.

It was perfect.

~

4:30 PM - THE STABLES

After cookies and cocoa and stories, Santa walked to the stables alone.

The sun was already setting. This far north, in late December, daylight was brief and precious.

The sky was painted in shades of purple and gold.

Rudolph stood in his stall, nose glowing softly, watching Santa approach.

"Hey, old friend," Santa said.

Hey yourself.

"I owe you an apology. A bigger one than I gave on Christmas Eve."

You already apologized.

"I know. But I need to say it again. I need you to know—really know—that I see you. That I've always seen you. That your light..." Santa's voice caught. "Your light has guided me through more darkness than I can count. And I'm sorry I ever made you feel like you needed to prove that. Like you needed to be anything other than exactly what you are."

Rudolph was quiet for a moment.

Then: *You were scared.*

"I was."

Of not mattering. Of being invisible. Of doing all this work and having no one see it.

"Yes."

I get that. I've been the weird one my whole life. The different one. The one who didn't fit. I wanted to matter too.

"You do matter. You matter so much."

I know. And you know what I learned? Rudolph stepped closer. Touched his nose to Santa's hand. *I matter whether they see it or not. My light is real whether they believe in it or not. And the same is true for you.*

Santa stroked Rudolph's neck. The fur was warm. Real. Here.

"How'd you get so wise?"

Seventy-three years of listening to you talk to yourself in the sleigh.

Santa laughed.

They stood together in the quiet. The stable warm. The hay soft. The world outside turning dark.

"Next year," Santa said, "no social media. No cameras. No proof. Just the work."

You sure?

"I'm sure. This week taught me something. The world doesn't need Santa's Instagram account. The world needs Santa. Just Santa. Showing up. Being real whether they believe it or not."

What about the algorithm? The surveillance concerns?

"Let them write their articles. Let them worry. We know the truth. We're watching because we care. Not because we're creeping. And the people who need us? They'll know. They've always known."

Rudolph's nose pulsed brighter. Agreement. Understanding.

Same time next year then.

"Same time next year."

But this time we fly in peace. No cameras. No comments. Just us and the work.

"Just us and the work," Santa agreed.

He left Rudolph to his hay. Walked back through the snow toward the workshop. The northern lights were starting—early tonight, as if the sky itself was celebrating.

Green and purple ribbons dancing.

A show seen by almost no one.

Magnificent regardless.

5:00 PM - THE VIDEO'S IMPACT

In homes around the world, people were watching.

The video had reached 15 million views. The comments were something Jinglebert had never seen before.

Not arguments about whether it was real.

Not analysis of pixels and deepfakes.

Just... recognition.

@TechBro9000: 8 hours searching for one photo. That's not AI. That's love.

@SkibidiRizzler: you saved that photo TWENTY-TWO YEARS AGO. You knew we'd need it. How did you KNOW?

@ConspiracyKevin: I spent 7 years searching for patterns in chaos. You spent 8 hours searching for proof of love. One of us was doing it right.

@MomOf4KidsNoSleep: Someone noticed I was tired. Someone SAW me. Someone cared enough to reach out to my kids and give them permission to help. That's not technology. That's human. That's REAL.

@LittleTimmy_Age7: see i told you. the real santa just shows up. thats all.

And then, at 5:47 PM, a new comment appeared.

From @SantaClausReal_Official2. Frank. Ohio Santa.

I've worked with kids for 12 years. Know what I learned? The magic isn't in proving you're real. It's in showing up. In seeing them. In remembering their names and their stories and their fears. In CARING when no one else does. @NaughtyOrNice—you showed us all what that looks like. Not just the kids. All of us. Thank you for the reminder. And for the job. I start January 1st. Dreams really do come true when someone believes in you.

Under his comment, thousands of replies:

this made me cry

12 years of showing up

that's the real magic

we're all just trying to be santa for someone

The conversation had shifted.

Not about whether Santa was real.

About what being "Santa" meant.

About showing up. About seeing people. About caring when it's hard. About searching for eight hours to find one photo because that one person matters.

About love as work.

About magic as attention.

About Christmas as a choice to SEE people who need to be seen.

Santa—the real one, sitting in his workshop eating cookies with his wife—didn't know any of this yet.

Wouldn't know until tomorrow.

But it was happening.

The transfiguration was complete.

6:00 PM - THE WINDOW

Santa stood at his office window. Same window. Same view. Same stars coming out.

But something was different.

He felt different.

Lighter. Clearer. More himself than he'd been in decades.

The phone sat on his desk behind him. Silent. He hadn't checked it since this morning.

Maybe he would tomorrow.

Maybe he wouldn't.

It didn't matter anymore.

The work was done. The people who needed him had been seen. The evidence had been shared.

And whether 15 million people believed him or 15 people believed him...

He was still real.

Still here.

Still showing up.

Mrs. Claus came to stand beside him. Slipped her hand into his.

"What are you thinking about?" she asked.

"Timmy," Santa said. "That seven-year-old who figured out what took me seventeen hundred years to understand."

"What's that?"

"That real things don't need proof. They just need to show up."

"And?"

"And I showed up. Did the work. Saw the people who needed seeing. Loved the ones who needed loving. Whether anyone believed it or not..." He smiled. "I showed up."

Mrs. Claus leaned her head on his shoulder.

"I'm proud of you."

"For what?"

"For finding your way back. For remembering what matters. For choosing the work over the applause."

They stood together in the window. The northern lights dancing outside. The workshop humming with post-Christmas energy below.

Somewhere, Marcus was having dinner with both his parents.

Somewhere, Danny was hugging his sister for the first time in five years.

Somewhere, Sarah was soaking in a bathtub while her children did the dishes.

Somewhere, Kevin was looking at photos and crying healing tears.

Somewhere, Timmy was crossing another day off his calendar.

All of it happening.

All of it real.

All of it because someone had shown up.

"Same time next year?" Santa asked.

"Same time next year," Mrs. Claus confirmed.

"No social media."

"No social media."

"No cameras."

"No cameras."

"Just the work."

"Just the work."

Santa turned from the window. Looked at his wife. At this woman who'd believed in him through everything. Who'd seen him when he couldn't see himself.

"I love you," he said.

"I love you too."

"Thank you for not giving up on me. When I forgot. When I doubted. When I thought I needed the world to tell me I mattered. Thank you for knowing better."

"You're welcome. Though I didn't do it alone. A seven-year-old boy helped."

Santa laughed. "Yes. Yes he did."

They walked out of the office together. Left the phone on the desk. Left the window. Left the view.

Because the work wasn't in watching.

The work was in doing.

In living.

In being present with the people who mattered.

In showing up.

Always.

~

7:00 PM - THE FINAL SCENE

Dinner in the great hall. The whole workshop family together.

Elves and reindeer and Mrs. Claus and Santa.

Torbin told stories about the year's builds. Greta shared updates on the reindeer herd. Buttons unveiled her newest cookie recipe. Jingle-bert—shyly—admitted he'd been writing poetry.

"Poetry?" Santa raised an eyebrow.

"About... about what it means to work behind the scenes. To do things no one sees. To matter without applause."

"Can I hear one?"

Jinglebert blushed. But he pulled out a small notebook. Read in a voice that shook at first, then grew stronger:

"We count the numbers,

We track the trends,

We measure engagement

That never ends.

But somewhere between

The metrics and views,

We forgot to count

What we might lose—

The quiet joy

Of work well done,

The gift of showing

Up for one,

Not a million,

Not a trending mass,

But one small child

Who needed us.

The numbers lie.

The work is true.

The magic isn't views—

It's you.

Showing up.

Being real.

Choosing love

Over how people feel

About whether you're true,

Or fake, or myth.

You're real to the ones

You showed up with.

And that's enough.

That has to be.

Not metrics. Not applause.

Just: I see."

The hall was silent.

Then Torbin started clapping. Slowly. Then faster.

Buttons joined. Then Greta. Then Mrs. Claus.

Then every elf in the hall.

And Santa—who hadn't cried in public since 1847—wiped his eyes and stood.

"That," he said, voice thick, "is the truest thing I've heard in seventeen hundred years."

Jinglebert smiled. "I learned from the best."

"No," Santa said. "You learned what I forgot. You figured it out faster than I did. And that..." He looked around the hall. At all these faces. These beings who'd chosen to spend their lives making Christmas happen. Who showed up every single day. Who worked in the dark. Who mattered whether anyone saw them or not.

"That makes you all the real magic. Not me. You."

"We're a team," Mrs. Claus said firmly. "All of us. Together. That's how it works."

"Together," Santa agreed.

They raised their mugs. Hot cocoa for everyone.

"To the work," Santa said.

"To the work," they echoed.

"To showing up."

"To showing up."

"To being real whether anyone believes it or not."

"To being real."

They drank.

Outside, the northern lights danced on.

Inside, the family celebrated.

And somewhere—on a phone in an office, on a desk by a window—15 million people were learning what Santa had learned:

That magic isn't proving you're real.

Magic is BEING real.

Showing up.

Seeing people.

Caring when it costs something.

Searching for eight hours to find one photo.

Driving three hours to hug your sister.

Booking your mom a spa day.

Opening old albums and crying healing tears.

Counting down twenty days with absolute faith.

The magic was always there.

In the work.

In the love.

In the showing up.

Always.

CHAPTER 13
"THE LIGHT STILL TRAVELS"

~

December 27th - January 15th - Time Passing

~

DECEMBER 28TH

Marcus's kitchen, 9:47 AM.

His parents sat at the table with a calendar spread between them. Real paper calendar, the kind with boxes big enough to write in.

"April 14th?" his dad asked.

His mom traced the date with her finger. "It's a Saturday. Spring. Not too hot yet. The garden will be blooming."

"The garden you keep saying you're going to plant?"

She smiled. A real smile. The kind Marcus hadn't seen in years. "The garden I'm GOING to plant. This time. I promise."

"I'll help," his dad said.

"You will?"

"Yeah. I will."

Marcus listened from the living room. Pretending to be on his phone. Actually just... listening.

His parents planning something together. Making promises they might actually keep.

It wasn't fixed. They'd had another argument last night about whose turn it was to take out the trash. This morning his dad had slept on the couch again.

But they were trying.

Really trying.

"Marcus!" his mom called. "Come here, please."

He walked to the kitchen. Stood in the doorway.

Both his parents looked at him. Together.

"We're renewing our vows," his dad said. "April 14th. And we want you to be our best man. Both of us. If that's... if that's okay."

Marcus's throat tightened.

"Yeah," he managed. "Yeah, that's okay."

His mom stood. Hugged him. Then his dad joined.

All three of them standing in the kitchen, holding each other, crying a little, laughing a little.

A family.

Not perfect.

But trying.

And that was enough.

DECEMBER 30TH

Coffee shop in Portland, 2:15 PM.

Danny sat at a corner table, leg bouncing, checking his phone every thirty seconds.

Then the door opened.

Emily.

Same face. Different. Older. Tired. Beautiful.

Their eyes met.

Five years of silence collapsed into nothing.

She walked over. Sat down. Neither of them spoke.

Just looked.

"Hi," Danny said finally.

"Hi," Emily said.

Then they both started crying.

Reached across the table. Held hands.

"I missed you," Danny said.

"I missed you too."

"I'm sorry."

"Me too."

"Can we just—" Danny's voice broke. "Can we just start over?"

Emily squeezed his hands. "I'd like that."

The barista brought Emily's coffee without her ordering. Danny had texted ahead. Remembered her order. Vanilla latte, extra shot, oat milk.

She noticed. Smiled through tears.

"You remembered."

"I never forgot."

They talked for four hours. About everything. About nothing. About the five years they'd lost and the rest of their lives they wouldn't.

At 6:47 PM, Emily said: "I'm getting married. May 17th. I want you there. Not just there—I want you to be my best man. If you—"

"Yes," Danny said immediately. "Yes. Absolutely yes."

"You don't even know him yet."

"If you love him, I'll love him. That's how this works."

Emily started crying again. "How did we lose five years?"

"Doesn't matter. We found them again."

Outside, it started to rain. Neither of them moved to leave.

They had time now.

All the time in the world.

～

JANUARY 3RD

The spa, 11:00 AM.

Sarah lay on the massage table, eyes closed, trying to remember the last time someone had touched her with the sole purpose of making her feel better.

She couldn't remember.

The masseuse's hands worked knots Sarah didn't know she had. Years of tension. Years of holding everything together. Years of being strong.

"You're very tense," the masseuse said gently.

"I'm a mom of four."

"Ah. Say no more."

They both laughed.

Sarah's phone buzzed in her bag across the room. She'd promised herself she wouldn't check it. The kids were fine. Her husband had them. They'd planned activities. Made a schedule. They were FINE.

But she still wanted to check.

"Your phone can wait," the masseuse said, reading her mind. "This is your time."

"I know, but—"

"No buts. When's the last time you put yourself first?"

Sarah was quiet.

"Exactly. So lie here. Breathe. Let someone take care of YOU for once."

Sarah closed her eyes.

Breathed.

Let go.

And cried. Not sad crying. Relief crying. The kind that comes when you finally, finally let someone else carry the weight.

"That's it," the masseuse said softly. "Let it out. You've earned this."

Sarah did.

And for the first time in years, she felt seen.

Not as Mom.

Not as Wife.

As Sarah.

Just Sarah.

And that was enough.

~

JANUARY 6TH, TUESDAY, 7:00 PM

Community center, folding chairs in a circle.

Kevin sat in the doorway. Had been sitting there for ten minutes. Watching.

Eight people in the circle. Different ages. Different stories. Same pain.

The facilitator looked up. Saw him. Smiled.

"You coming in?"

Kevin's hands were shaking.

"Yeah," he said. "Yeah, I'm coming in."

He walked to the circle. Sat in an empty chair.

Everyone looked at him. Not judging. Just... seeing.

"Welcome," the facilitator said. "First time?"

Kevin nodded.

"Want to introduce yourself?"

"I'm Kevin. And I..." He stopped. Took a breath. "I lost my parents seven years ago. In a fire. And I've been angry ever since. At everyone. At everything. At the universe for taking them." His voice cracked. "But I'm tired of being angry. I'm tired of seeing patterns in chaos. I'm tired of conspiracy theories and red string and... and not living."

He looked around the circle. At these strangers who understood.

"I just want to remember the good things. The real things. The love that existed before the fire. Is that..." His voice got smaller. "Is that okay?"

A woman across the circle—maybe forty, kind eyes—smiled through tears.

"That's not just okay," she said. "That's everything. That's the whole point."

Kevin nodded. Couldn't speak.

"We're glad you're here," the facilitator said.

"Me too," Kevin whispered.

And for the first time in seven years, he meant it.

JANUARY 10TH

Children's hospital, pediatric oncology wing, 10:00 AM.

Frank walked through the doors in his new Santa suit. Professional quality. Perfect fit. The hospital had paid for it.

"SANTA!" A little girl's voice. Emma. Six years old. Acute lymphoblastic leukemia.

Frank knelt beside her bed. "Hey, Emma. How you feeling today?"

"Tired. But you're here, so that's good."

"I'll always be here. Every Tuesday and Thursday. You can count on it."

"Promise?"

"Promise."

Emma's mom stood in the corner, crying quietly. Frank met her eyes. She mouthed: *Thank you.*

He spent two hours making rounds. Knew every kid's name. Knew their diagnoses. Knew what they were fighting. Knew what they needed to hear.

Not "you'll be okay."

Sometimes they wouldn't be okay.

But "I see you. You're not alone. You matter."

That they could always believe.

At noon, Dr. Martinez found him in the hallway.

"You're good at this," she said.

"I've had practice."

"Twelve years, I heard."

Frank nodded. "Twelve years of showing up. Whether anyone noticed or not."

"Someone noticed," Dr. Martinez said. She handed him a badge. His photo. His name. Title: Child Life Specialist.

Frank held it. Stared.

"This is real?" His voice shook.

"Very real. You start full-time next Monday. Welcome to the team, Frank."

He couldn't speak. Just nodded. Held the badge like it might disappear.

Dr. Martinez smiled. "Dreams really do come true when someone believes in you."

Frank laughed. Cried. Both.

"Yeah," he said. "Yeah, they do."

JANUARY 15TH, 3:47 PM

Airport arrivals terminal.

Timmy bounced on his toes. Literally bounced. Couldn't stay still if his life depended on it.

"When's his plane landing?" He'd asked this seventeen times.

"Any minute, baby." His mom squeezed his hand.

"Any minute?"

"Any minute."

Timmy held his sign higher. Construction paper and markers and glitter glue. WELCOME HOME DAD!!! Three exclamation points. He'd been very specific about three.

"There!" His mom pointed.

Soldiers emerging from the gate. Tired. Dirty. Home.

Timmy scanned faces. Looking. Searching. WHERE WAS—

"THERE! MOM, THERE!"

He was running before she could stop him.

Full sprint.

"DAD!"

His father dropped his duffel bag. Fell to his knees. Arms open.

Timmy crashed into him. Both of them crying. Both of them laughing.

"You're home! You're REAL! You're HOME!"

"I'm home, buddy. I'm home."

His mom reached them. Joined the hug. All three of them on the airport floor, holding each other, crying, complete.

"Santa said you were coming," Timmy said into his dad's shoulder. "He PROMISED."

His dad pulled back. Looked at him. "Santa, huh?"

"Yeah. He came. He's real. And he told me you were coming home January 15th and he was RIGHT."

His father looked at his mother over Timmy's head. She nodded. Smiled through tears.

"Then I guess Santa knows what he's talking about," his dad said.

"He always does," Timmy said confidently. "Because he SHOWS UP. That's what real people do."

His father held him tighter.

"Yeah, buddy. Yeah, they do."

~

JANUARY 16TH - NORTH POLE

The @NaughtyOrNice account sat dark.

Still there. Still verified. But dormant.

Waiting.

Not for engagement. Not for metrics.

Just... existing. Real whether anyone looked at it or not.

In the workshop, letters arrived. Not like the Christmas rush. Slower. Steadier.

But different letters now.

Mrs. Claus sorted them while Santa worked at his desk, already planning for next December.

"Kris?" she said. "You should read these."

He looked up. "What kind?"

"The new kind."

Santa took the pile. Read the first one:

Dear Santa,

I don't need toys. I just feel lonely at school. Does anyone see me?

Love, Maya (age 8)

The second:

Dear Santa,

My parents fight and it scares me. Can you help them remember why they got married?

Love, Jason (age 11)

The third:

Dear Santa,

I'm sad and I don't know why. Is that okay? Can you still see me even if I don't know what's wrong?

Love, Sophie (age 9)

Santa read them all. Every one. Twenty-three letters. All asking the same thing in different ways:

Do I matter? Does anyone see me? Am I alone?

He looked at Mrs. Claus.

"They learned," he said quietly.

"What did they learn?"

"To ask for what they really need. Not toys. Connection. To be seen. To matter."

Mrs. Claus smiled. "And will you answer them?"

"Every one," Santa said. "I'll answer every single one."

He pulled out paper. His pen. Started writing.

Dear Maya,

I see you. You're not alone. I promise...

THE WORKSHOP

Torbin at his bench, building next year's toys. Already innovating. Already creating.

Greta in the stables, tending to reindeer. Rudolph's nose glowing steady, a lighthouse in the dark.

Buttons in the kitchen, testing new cookie recipes. "This one needs more salt. And love. Definitely more love."

Jinglebert at his computer, but not checking metrics. Writing poetry. About work. About showing up. About mattering whether anyone sees you or not.

The work continuing.

As it always had.

As it always would.

Because that's what real things do.

They persist.

~

THAT NIGHT

Santa and Mrs. Claus in bed. Stars visible through the window. Northern lights dancing silent green.

"Same time next year?" she asked.

"Same time next year," he confirmed.

"No social media."

"No social media."

"Just the work."

"Just the work."

She turned off the light. Darkness. Starlight.

"Kris?"

"Yeah?"

"I'm proud of you. For learning. For remembering. For choosing the work over the applause."

"I had good teachers. A seven-year-old. A wife. A whole family reminding me what mattered."

"We all need reminders sometimes."

"Yeah. We do."

They lay in silence. The kind of comfortable silence that comes after four hundred years of marriage.

Then Santa spoke into the dark:

"The gifts keep giving."

"What?"

"Something I realized. When you show up for someone—really show up, really see them—the gift keeps giving. Marcus will remember. Danny will remember. Sarah will remember. Kevin. Timmy. They'll carry it forward. They'll show up for someone else. The light keeps traveling."

Mrs. Claus squeezed his hand. "Like starlight."

"Exactly like starlight."

Outside their window, the universe continued its ancient work. Stars burning light years away. That light traveling through space, through time, reaching earth long after the source had died.

Still beautiful.

Still real.

Still shining.

Somewhere, a child was typing.

Late at night. Parents asleep. Opening a laptop.

Dear Santa,

Thank you for seeing me. I don't need toys. I just needed to know someone cares. You showed me someone does. Now I can be someone who cares too. Thank you.

Love, [name]

SEND

~

North Pole, workshop, printer activating.

Letter printing.

Falling into the pile.

Santa would read it tomorrow.

Or the next day.

Or the next.

But he'd read it.

He reads them all.

THE FINAL THOUGHT

Santa stared at the ceiling. Mrs. Claus breathing softly beside him. Sleep pulling him down.

But one thought remained, clear as stars:

Somewhere, a star's light is traveling.

From a source long dead.

Still shining.

Still reaching earth.

Still beautiful.

Still REAL.

Some lights travel longer than their source lives.

Some love outlasts the lover.

Some magic transcends the magician.

His eyes closed.

His breathing slowed.

His last conscious thought:

See you next year.

And then: sleep.

Dreamless.

Earned.

Peace.

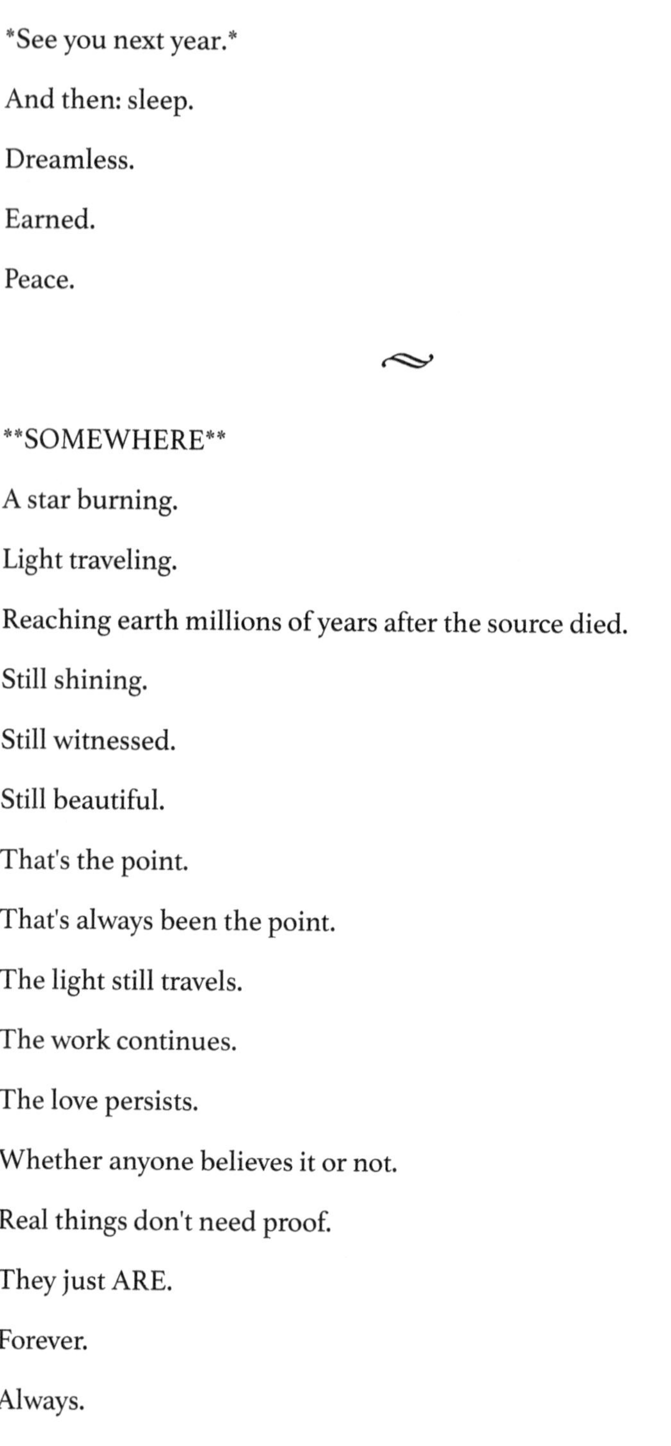

SOMEWHERE

A star burning.

Light traveling.

Reaching earth millions of years after the source died.

Still shining.

Still witnessed.

Still beautiful.

That's the point.

That's always been the point.

The light still travels.

The work continues.

The love persists.

Whether anyone believes it or not.

Real things don't need proof.

They just ARE.

Forever.

Always.

Real.

THE END

For everyone who shows up. For everyone who sees. For everyone who loves when it costs something. For everyone who works in the dark. You are the real magic. Thank you.*